Greek Millionaire, Unruly Wife

SUN CHARA

A division of HarperCollins*Publishers*
www.harpercollins.co.uk

Harper*Impulse* an imprint of
HarperCollins*Publishers*
1 London Bridge Street
London SE1 9GF

www.harpercollins.co.uk

First published in Great Britain in ebook format by
Harper*Impulse* 2017

A catalogue record for this book
is available from the British Library

ISBN: 9780008240639

This novel is entirely a work of fiction.
The names, characters and incidents portrayed in it are
the work of the author's imagination. Any resemblance to
actual persons, living or dead, events or localities is
entirely coincidental.

Set in Minion by Palimpsest Book Production Limited,
Falkirk, Stirlingshire

Printed and bound in Great Britain

Unlimited thanks to my wonderful brother, Harry, who is one in a million … believe the best is yet to be!

Chapter 1

"I'll take that one."

"The green gown, *Monsieur* Leonadis?"

"No, the model."

The man chuckled. "The model's not for sale, *monsieur*."

"You wanna bet?" Michalis Leonadis loosened his tie, lifted an arrogant eyebrow at the sales manager of the Haute Couture show in Paris, and geared up for battle … not with the manager but … with her. Tracking the model every step with his slitted gaze, he slipped a hand inside the pocket of his jacket and extracted a card, then a pen.

Julia, strutting down the runway and steaming up the ballroom in the Hôtel de Crillon had cost him a marriage, and a billion dollars in a Tokyo deal gone belly-up. As if that hadn't been enough, his head of security informed him she'd recently given—

Applause broke out, splintering his thoughts, and spiking his fury … his passion. For revenge.

She'd ripped his heart out. Shredded his pride. Cost him.

Her untimely exit had rocked his sphere and his bank account. She nearly bankrupted him. He'd put everything on hold to search for her, and to clean up the legal mess his uncle's *amour* had created when she'd charmed … er … scammed the old guy into signing half the Leonadis fortune to her and ultimately her heir. The fortune Michalis had slaved over years to amass.

He set his jaw, batted that distraction from his mind, and turned his laser sharp eyes back to the supermodel, his present dilemma.

When he found out Julia had been living it up in Paris, he'd shut her out, and scrambled to salvage his business and stay afloat—he'd waste no more time on her. He was better off without her.

A spike lodged in his aorta, but he ignored the sting.

He clamped his teeth, his breath rumbling in his chest and escaping through his nose in a hostile sound. How dare she keep *that* a secret from him?

Cold, calculating bi— the expletive stinging his tongue was smothered by shouts of "*Brava!*" from the audience.

He scrawled a message on his business card, adrenaline pumping him to action.

She'd definitely pay. He curled his lip. His way.

Michalis slapped the card in the man's hand. "Make sure she gets it."

The man glanced at the bold insignia of the Leonadis Cruise Line on the card and inclined his head. "*Oui*, Monsieur Leonadis."

Michalis tuned him out.

He liked things simple. She'd been anything but.

He liked to keep his focus razor-sharp, his mind alert, his instinct in play and quantum leap over his competition. That biz acumen had held him in good stead when, years ago, he'd taken over his uncle's run-down tourist boat rentals in Athens and built it into a mega international shipping line. At thirty-eight he still thrived on the thrill, the challenge. Julia'd been that, and he'd conquered her resistance, caught her; an unbidden smile skimmed his mouth, then morphed into a snarl.

He'd given her everything—he'd given her the world. And in

return, at the first sign of rough waters, she'd jumped ship and created a tidal wave of confusion.

But now, she looked none the worse for it. And that rankled his ego.

The stylist had swept her sun-bleached hair up, and the dresser had fitted her into a body-hugging gown, matching her eyes and the emeralds dangling from her ears. The high collar and flared hem, a demure contrast to her sultry gaze, pouty mouth, and the sway of her hips as she worked the catwalk.

Worked the room.

Cool. Sexy. Seductive.

The male clientele salivated and the women gasped in admiration.

He smirked. So much for the sophisticated façade of the VIPs who'd flocked to the fashion extravaganza. His smirk turned into a guffaw. She'd gotten to them ... engaged their imagination ... triggering fantasies and loosening purse strings.

He should know. His already rock hard abs tensed. She'd gotten under his skin ... his psyche. Shaking his head, he chuckled; an empty sound. Past tense ... *had*. No more. The padlock on his heart and ice in his veins proved it.

He'd not end up a stooge like his uncle.

Nodding to the man holding his business card, Michalis strode to the exit, but couldn't resist tossing her another glance over his shoulder.

A hot babe. He jutted his chin. A classy stunner. That's what had attracted him in the first place—amusement tugged the corner of his lips. How did she manage to walk on those high heels? He shrugged, about to continue on his way, but then braked to a stop.

She paused, pivoted. And the fur stole slipped from her shoulders, the edgy cut of the neckline plunging to the small of her back.

His chest tightened, his hand fisted, a growl built in his throat.

Beneath the stage lights, her bare back gleamed smooth, flawless ... and his fingers tingled, his memory kindling. He'd touched her ... her skin hot beneath his fingers ... his mouth nibbling down to the curve of her hip—he ground his teeth, his pulse thudding—he'd cupped her buttocks, turned her over, her breasts scorching his chest, his mouth on hers ... she'd wrapped her legs around him, holding him close, and he had thrust deep inside her—

A crescendo of sound from the band splintered his erotic fantasy, and he blinked, gulping the growl away.

She inched off a long glove, tossed it to the audience and did the same with the other, to the eruption of wolf whistles. Then, dismissing her admirers with a quirk of an eyebrow, she placed a hand on her hip and sauntered away, the stole trailing at her feet. At the top of the ramp, she paused, glanced over her shoulder, hinted a smile, winked and disappeared back stage to deafening applause and cheers of, "*Encore!*"

Michalis grazed his jaw with his knuckles.

Her signals were practiced and unmistakable. Luring ... snaring ... vanishing.

She'd played that game on him, and every cell in his body sizzled with desire, but his mind defied the temptation.

The sensation warring inside him could be nothing more than his determination to recoup what belonged to him. What she'd stolen from him. He curled his lip in contempt and stomped from the ballroom, his pulse drilling into his ribs. His every move had to be a tactical *tour de force* to ensure a victory.

"*Merci beaucoup.*" Julia kicked off her shoes and thanked the wardrobe girl helping her from the gown, the chiffon a caress upon her skin.

Unclipping the emeralds from her ears, she set them on the dresser, and a sigh struggled from deep inside her. Not long ago, she'd owned countless such designer gowns, shoes, jewelry, and had the man—the life—to go with it. A sound gurgled in her throat, and the girl cast her an odd look. Julia swallowed and turned away, blinking back the tears pressing against her lids.

In just three months, her dreams had soured, her fairytale marriage to the Greek billionaire fractured, but—a tremulous smile traced her mouth—she hadn't come away empty handed.

She pulled a sweater over her head and slipped into her jeans, sucking in her tummy to get the zipper and snap to work. She grimaced. A few more pounds still to lose, but with the tricks of the trade, she managed to fit into the designer threads. Unclipping her hair, she fluffed it with her fingers, let it fall to her shoulders and rubbed her scalp with her fingertips. A hint of hairspray tainted the air. She twitched her nose and glanced in the mirror. Her makeup would have to wait 'til she got home.

"Ah, *chéri*."

She glanced up from slipping on her ankle boots and smiled. "Hey, Chachee, how'd it go?"

"*Magnifique!*" He kissed the tips of his fingers for emphasis.

"Of course, what else for Chachee Originals?" She grinned, plunked her wool beret on her head, grabbed her jacket and shoulder bag. "Brr." She mocked a shiver. "Paris in the spring might be the stuff of dreams, but it's freezing today."

"Doesn't have to be, *chéri*," he teased, wiggling his pierced brow. "You have an admirer."

"You're terrific at boosting a girl's confidence, Charles." She smiled and stepped toward the exit sign above the door. "But I gotta go."

"Worth checking this one out."

"Some other time." A man wasn't her priority right now, not since Michalis—a pang pierced her heart, and she shook her head, dispelling the taunting image. Michalis Leonadis had been her

11

colossal blunder, and she wouldn't think about him. Not now. Not ever.

"Oh, no." Charles slapped a hand on his forehead and another against his heart in mock despair.

She laughed, and he put the card in her palm, folding her fingers over it.

"I'd go for him myself but—" He winked.

She laughed the louder, for Charles was as straight as they came, with a wife and a couple of kids. But his flamboyant style: blue locks and bejeweled hands, often gave rise to rumors in this highly-strung, fast-paced fashion industry. So, he nipped them in the bud with his brash repartee.

"But since I won't—" He took her by the shoulders, spun her around, and gave her a nudge out the door "—how 'bout you go check him out?"

"I can't, Chach," she said. "I gotta get home."

He shrugged, walked past her and raising a hand, pointed toward the lobby.

"Oh, okay, I'll take a peek on my way out."

His chuckle echoed back to her. It brought a twitch of amusement to her lips, and then she sobered. She owed him a debt of gratitude. If he hadn't booked her on the show, she wouldn't have made the month's rent. At twenty-eight, and having been away from the fashion circuit for over a year, modeling opportunities were few and far between.

Walking down the hallway, she looped the strap of her purse over her shoulder and opened her hand. She glanced at the card and got socked in the stomach. A gasp shot from her mouth. Her head spun, her limbs shook, and her pulse raced. The familiar signature zoomed in and out of focus. *8 p.m. Le Bar. ML.* Bold, direct, like the man.

What was Michalis Leonadis doing on her doorstep after a year's silence?

Perspiration oozed from her every pore, making her sweater

stick to her skin even in the air-conditioned corridor. Michalis Leonadis, the man she'd loved, once … and the man she now hated with every fiber of her being.

What did he *want*? Shivers iced her skin. What did he *know*?

Chapter 2

Could he know about—?

"Dear God, no." Fear squeezed her heart, and her mouth felt thick with sawdust. A tremor ripped through her, and she collapsed against the wall, hyperventilating.

Julia choked down the bile rising in her throat and rushed into the bathroom. Gripping the counter, she leaned over the sink and sucked in mouthfuls of air, stemming the chills frisking her body. She twisted the faucet open, splashed water on her face and glanced in the wall-length mirror, the paleness of her skin evident even beneath her makeup.

"Michalis Leonadis." His name fizzed between her teeth, acid on her tongue. She'd given him her heart, her body ... everything, and he'd trampled on it. A whimper sounded from deep in her throat, and haunting memories flooded her mind ...

"Michalis *mou*," she'd called, unlocking the door of their Athens penthouse. The breathtaking view of the Aegean Sea always brought a lift to her heart and a smile to her face; but it was nothing compared to the joy bursting in her heart from the doctor's news that she wanted to share with her husband of three months.

"*Agape mou*, you're back early." He walked from the bathroom barefoot, drying his hair with a towel, another towel tied around his hips. A dash of dark hair plastered to his sculpted chest, a sexy smile on his mouth.

Breath caught in her throat, her heart skipped, her stomach dipped.

This sexy hunk was hers. She smiled, and started to run to him.

The bedroom door opened and her step faltered, the smile wiped from her face.

"Michalis *mou*." The woman giggled, tying the sash of a terry towel robe over the skimpiest of negligees. She teetered toward him on high-heeled slippers and stumbled into his arms. "I don't think this is such a good idea, even for the honeym—"

"Apparently not," Julia said, the words crackling from her frozen lips. She shot Michalis a lethal look. "You got caught." Every nerve in her body twittered, and she swayed, but managed to stand her ground, her gaze darting from her husband to the other woman.

She couldn't fathom the scene before her eyes. She blinked. Swallowed. Perhaps she'd wake up from this nightmare.

"I was going to tell you—" The words dissolved in his throat, and he narrowed his gaze, the navy flecks in his eyes darkening.

Julia staggered back a step and seized the door handle before she slithered to the carpet. Raw pain must've surfaced on her features, for he stepped toward her, the scent of his cologne stinging the gouge inside her.

She held up one hand, shaking her head.

"It's not what you—" He glanced at his guest, and scrubbed his shaven cheek with his fist.

"I'm sorry," the woman murmured, tripping back into the bedroom.

He nodded. "Julia—"

She backed away. At least it had been in the guestroom and

not their bedroom … on their bed. For some perverse reason, the thought gashed her mind. A hysterical laugh bubbled in her throat, and she flew out the door.

The streets of Athens buzzed with activity. Shoppers, tourists and locals sat at outside *tavernas*, sampling *souvlaki*, *spanakopita* while others sipped Greek coffee, Coca-Cola or *ouzo*, the licorice flavored liquor. *Bouzouki* music serenaded to the blaring of horns and irate taxi drivers gesturing out the windows at other drivers.

Laughter. Life everywhere.

But Julia felt dead … except for the life growing inside her.

Aimlessly, she wandered the narrow roads, ignoring his mobile calls and ditching the chauffeur he'd sicced on her. Somehow, she made her way past the outdoor market and to the beach. She meandered through the crowds of sunbathers to a secluded patch beneath a eucalyptus tree. Hours drifted by, and she sat there, gazing out to sea, praying for an answer. The sea breeze cooled her cheeks, and by the time the sun turned the sky into a kaleidoscope of color, the initial shock had worn off.

At last, she came to a decision and picked up his next call.

"I'm flying back from the Mykonos office," he said, his words cool through the airwaves. "We'll discuss it tonight."

"What time?" she murmured, detached … numb.

"It'll be late because—"

She hung up, sickened by his betrayal.

An hour later, she'd packed, called a cab and headed for Athens International Airport, jetting out of his life …

Now, he'd blasted back into her life in Paris, and she wondered why.

But it didn't matter. Her wounds had healed, and Michalis Leonadis could go jump in the Mediterranean for all she cared. She crumpled his card in her hand and was about to trash it when a couple of girls burst into the ladies room, their chatter shattering her thoughts.

Julia made her exit, biting her lip. Maybe it should matter to her. Michalis Leonadis did everything with purpose. Her throat constricted and her temples throbbed. Angst stabbed. She drew in a breath and eased up. There was no way he could know. None.

But just to be sure, she rummaged in her purse for her cell and called home, her matchbox-sized one-bedroom pad. "Mrs. Knightley, I may be a bit late tonight." A pause. "Did anyone visit today?" A sigh of relief filtered from her mouth. "No? Okay."

Michalis Leonadis did not know her secret. And he wouldn't know. She pressed her lips tight, but her shoulders slumped. One day she'd have to tell him … and tell Amy about her father.

But not today.

Today was about leveling the playing field. She'd go and see why he was here, why he sought her out after a year's silence. The battle lines had been drawn … the divorce would be final when he signed the papers. And he could do that from Greece via his solicitor.

She crinkled her brow. Did he think she'd take him to the cleaners? A brittle sound broke from her lips. Her eyes misted. She wanted nothing from him except what he'd already given her.

Bashing down the emotion, she steeled her nerves and walked across the atrium, each step a lead weight. She bypassed the crystal chandeliers, the needlepoint wall-hangings, the ornate furniture, the statues, and the opulent deco of this palatial Louis XVI historic hotel … but didn't see them.

Knowledge was power. She must stack her arsenal to trump the powerful Greek she'd married.

Her past folly. She shook her shoulders. But it would not become her present, and certainly not her future. She fumbled in her step, and a smile feathered her mouth. Her future waited at home.

A moment later, she stood outside the near empty *Le Bar*. The

17

fashion trendsetters would soon be descending to the delight of the cocktail waitresses waiting for customers and subsequent tips. Julia inhaled and exhaled several puffs of air, swiped her damp palms on her thighs, flicked a stray strand of hair off her shoulders and with her head held high marched into the intimately lit lounge. The melody from the pianist wrapped around her, soothing, but then turned abrasive.

She saw him.

A trickle of moisture between her breasts, her mouth went dry. He lounged at a table in the far corner of the room with drink in hand and clicked off a call on his phone.

Her heart thudded. Memories flooded her mind. Bittersweet, and she wished … but no, he'd destroyed everything they'd shared.

Destroyed her.

At that precise moment, he glanced her way, and the blue intensity of his eyes tacked her to the spot. Shockwaves ripped through her, rocking her world anew. She ground her teeth, determined not to feel anything for this man, except indifference.

The best defense was a good offense, so she stormed across the floor to his table. He at least had the good manners to stand up.

"Julia," he said, the deep timbre of his voice jolting her senses.

"Michalis," she murmured, her tone cool.

For a second or two neither one of them said anything, then he mocked a cough.

Resentment gnawed her insides. Not even a *hello* from him. This did not bode well.

"A drink?" he offered, motioning her to sit down.

"No thank you," she murmured, standing her ground.

He sat back down, noted her defiance and waved to the waitress. "A sparkling water with lime."

"You'll have to drink it, Michalis."

He hiked a brow, and sipped his bourbon on the rocks, his dark gaze glued on her. He only ever had one drink, max, of the

18

hard stuff. Discipline. He always wanted to be in control of his faculties.

She smirked. In charge of everything and everyone. Including her. She wondered if the control tactics extended to his family. Then she blinked, realizing she knew very little about the man she married. It had been a whirlwind romance, a spur of the moment wedding at Our Lady Tourliani Monastery on Mykonos.

Emotion surged inside her, nearly suffocating her. She drew in a breath and exhaled a breath. A celebrity style wedding loomed on the horizon afterward he'd hinted. Under his magnetic spell, like a fool, she believed him. But no more. The magic had vaporized.

Then why are you quaking, and why is your heart pounding? She ignored the self-inflicted taunt, and at that moment, her stomach rumbled. Mortified, she slapped her hand over her abdomen.

"Hungry?" He smiled, but it didn't reach his eyes.

"No." She'd skipped lunch and dinner to ensure she fit into the gowns, but seeing him again had made her lose her appetite. A sliver of a grin brushed her mouth. Something good might come out of this after all—a few lost pounds.

"Something amusing?" he asked, tone dry.

She shook her head and plunged into the depths. "Why are you here?"

He snared her in his sights. "Sit down and I'll tell you."

Chapter 3

Julia collapsed onto the velvet chair and licked her lips, the cherry flavor of her lipstick spiking her taste-buds.

He shuttered his eyes, his jaw granite hard, and his grip on the tumbler tightened.

"Okay, I'm sitting," she said, her tone defiant.

He remained silent and, swirling the liquid in his glass, kept her on tenterhooks. A delay maneuver? A control tactic?

Julia took the moment of reprieve to study him. A Ralph Lauren jacket framed his broad shoulders, the Trump original tie a contrast to the white shirt stretched across his chest. His chiseled features bespoke of his Greek ancestry, his skin tanned, his hands ... strong, capable, tender ... in the way he'd touched her, held her, stroked her ... loved her. Anguish tore through her. She'd laid her head on his chest, the swirl of hair tickling her cheek, his heart thundering in her ear ... but that had been a million years ago.

Before he—

A whimper built inside her, ready to burst from her mouth, but she couldn't let him see he still affected her. Too dangerous for her mind, her emotions, her world. She must remain immune to his charm, his magnetism, and his potent sexuality. The whimper came out like a near snort, and he shot her a glacial look.

"I-I can't stay," she murmured.

"You'll stay long enough." He leaned back, hitched up a trouser leg and crossed one leg over the other.

Cool. Powerful. Wealthy.

She reached for the drink he'd ordered, took a sip and the fizz tickled her nose, the taste of lime fresh upon her tongue. Slowly she set it back on the table, controlling the temptation to hurl it in his face. But only just.

Impeccable in his suit, he exuded a debonair flair of the lifestyle of the wealthy and the beautiful. She'd been the opposite. Casual and ordinary in jeans, halter-top and sandals, her sunburned nose magnifying her freckles. Except when the fashion pros worked their magic, transforming her into a human mannequin, and every man's fantasy.

"I deserve an answer, Michalis." She foolishly imagined he'd been captivated by the real her, not the plastic copy, but obviously she'd been wrong. Plastic deteriorated. And so had their marriage.

Jitters sprang inside her, and she cupped the water glass with her hands, the condensation cooling her palms. If he so easily trampled on their marriage vows, he'd just as easily demolish her life again … for no other reason than daring to challenge him … daring to leave him … daring to keep a secret.

"You do deserve an answer," he said, his tone cool, hard. "As I do."

"What do you mean?" She bolted upright, letting go of the glass and gripping the arms of the chair.

"Hit a nerve, have I?"

"I don't know what you're talking about?" she fired back, but didn't quite meet his eyes.

"Perhaps this'll refresh your memory, *yineka mou*."

"Don't call me that … I'm not your wife." Not if he could betray her like he had, the image branded her brain cells.

21

"Technically, you are—" He leveled her with a look that rammed her ribs into her backbone, squashing her heart. "—until the divorce papers are signed."

Her heart flipped, but then relief rushed through her. He didn't know. He was here because of the divorce.

She squinted at him. "You could've done that from Greece."

"What, and not see your beautiful face again?" he mocked. "You can have your divorce, Julia."

"Di-ivorce." The word grated her tongue like gravel. "Y-yes."

"But there is a penalty."

Her head snapped up, and she caught the stern set of his jaw, skin stretched taut across his cheekbones, the set of his mouth. His mouth had taught her such passion, created such erotic delight in her. His lips on hers, on her breast and gliding down her body, suckling her navel, and then lower to—Heaven.

Hell.

He knew.

She blinked, eclipsing the sensual images and crushing the memory beneath the gauntlet he tossed. Her freedom would come at a cost.

"I can't imagine what it is," she breathed out, sarcasm lacing her words, as the tremors inside her picked up momentum.

He laughed, a dry sound that sent chills up her spine.

A premonition … an astronomical price to pay.

"You can have your divorce, Julia." His eyes glittered an ice storm, and he shot straight into her heart. "In exchange for my daughter."

"No!" She leaped up so fast, the glass tipped over, liquid sloshing over the side onto the table. She couldn't care less.

"I'll see you in court then."

Blackness undulated before her eyes, her pulse vaulted into her throat and the wool of her sweater itched her damp-sweat skin. She couldn't beat Michalis Leonadis in a court of law … he had the money, the power, the connections. A bleat of sound from her mouth, and she gnashed it away, pulling on her inner strength that had gotten her through the last year. "I'll see you in hell first."

"That could be arranged," he muttered, his words flint hard.

"Wh-hat do you mean?"

"How long did you think you could keep this from me?" he baited, fury in his midnight blue eyes.

The eyes of a hunter cornering his prey … her.

"You dare keep my child from me, Julia?"

"I-I was going to tell—"

"Enough," he bit out. "Now sit down before you make a scene."

She sank in the chair and clasped her hands in her lap to stop their trembling, her mind whirling. "I won't let you take her away from me, Michalis."

He arched an aristocratic brow. "How do you propose to stop me?"

"I'll do whatever it takes."

"*Poli kala* … very well." A cold smile. "You will return with me to Greece for one month."

She shrank back in her chair, rejecting his words, but her heartbeat skipped and her body flamed with awareness. Shock—that must be it.

"Why?"

"Because I want to get to know my child," he ground out. "And a three-month-old needs her mother."

"Glad you recognize that fact."

"And her father."

As much as she resisted, Julia knew he was right, but couldn't help bouncing back with, "Amy can get to know you when she's older."

"Amy," he whispered, a flicker of tenderness in his eyes. "She'll get to know me now."

Her heart sank. "You can come and visit her here, Michalis." She was clutching at straws.

23

"And have you disappear again?" He picked up his glass, tossed the last of his drink down his throat and slammed the glass on the table. "We have things to discuss ... do." His gaze traveled over her, pausing at her breasts which were rising and falling with the over exertion of her lungs, a notch lower to the apex of her thighs, then back up to her face, her eyes, her mouth.

"No, Michalis."

"I will do what I please, when I please, how I please ... with you."

"No."

"Yes."

"I-I can't Michalis," she murmured, her voice breaking. "Not after you—"

"After I what, Julia?" he challenged, his words fueling white-hot anger.

"You made it clear you don't want me." She gripped her purse so hard, her fingers hurt. "And now I don't want you."

A shadow flittered across his eyes, and a muscle assaulted his jaw.

"You're a necessity for the child," he said, his tone reasonable. "While there you'll also entertain me."

"You can't have me," she bounded to her feet, finding her voice.

"I figured you might say that." He signed the bill for the drinks to his room and stood, his eyes an ocean tempest.

Of course he'd be staying here, she thought, the extravagant rates would not dent his bank account. He was welcome to his money. All she wanted was her daughter. A ferocity rose up inside her. She'd never abandon her child like she'd been abandoned. The memory was like a scar on her psyche. Then to have Michalis do the same to her was—

"My solicitor will be in touch," he bit out.

She blanched, a quake building inside her. There was no way she could fight him in court, she couldn't afford it.

"You'll have your divorce, Julia and I'll have my daughter."

24

"No, please," she gasped.

"Then you will agree to my terms."

She nodded, a void inside her. "A-a month, Michalis and not a day longer." Not an hour, minute, second. A huff of a breath, then a grit of sound, and she whacked him with her gaze. "I'll make every day I'm there hell for you."

He chuckled, but it sounded lifeless, exactly how she felt. She took a step past him.

"I'll send a car for you tomorrow at 8 a.m."

She kept walking, shutting him from her thoughts.

"One more thing, Julia."

She spun around, and her skin frosted. He stood there, tall, dark, remote. And sexy.

A lethal adversary.

To her heart … her mind … her life … her future.

"Don't even think of skipping town tonight." A cruel line carved his mouth. "I've security and—"

"You're despicable."

"Is that all?" He shrugged, but a nerve bashed his cheek. A moment of deliberation, and he delivered the blow that felled her. "You might have to explain to your daughter why your selfish actions nixed her billion-dollar inheritance."

"Have you no honor?"

"You dare speak to me of honor?" he snarled. "You, who slunk out behind my back?"

Every fiber in her body quivered, the quake about to erupt inside her, and she blinked the blur from her eyes, easing the pressure. "You'd really use our child as a bargaining chip?" she murmured.

A lock of hair flopped over his brow, his Adam's apple bopped, and his breath blasted from his nostrils like a snorting bull. "It's your move, Julia."

Her heart palpitated. By sleight of hand, he managed to immobilize her. She flexed her hands, breathed in and exhaled.

If she was going to gain her freedom and secure her daughter's financial future, she had to make a pact with this callous stranger before her. She'd be selling herself to him, and something seemed to die inside her.

"I won't let you jeopardize her future, Michalis," she fired, her words an ice blizzard.

"Then you'll be there tomorrow, ready to warm my bed."

Chapter 4

"Did you undress me, Michalis?" Julia, wearing a mid-thigh length robe and with tousled hair, stomped barefoot onto the terrace of the Leonadis villa overlooking the Mediterranean Sea.

"Did you want me to?" Amusement tugged at his mouth, and he set the newspaper he'd been reading on the table, his x-ray vision raking her head to toe.

"Don't be ridiculous." She clutched the robe closer about her body, and he laughed. And that had her ire rising ... as well as her temperature and heart rate.

"Is it?" He leaned back in his chair, his words a low rumble in his chest sent her emotions into a scramble.

"Answer me." She slid her fingers in her long locks and shoved them off her forehead. "Did you ... I mean did we ... you ... me—"

"Yes and no."

"What's that supposed to mean?"

"Coffee?" He picked up the *briki*, the coffee pot, and motioned her to sit down for breakfast.

"Don't change the subject."

An impatient sigh filtered from his mouth, and he took his time refilling his cup, then hers. "You were exhausted after the flight and conked out after putting Amy to bed." He raised the demitasse, took a long sip and reset it on the saucer. "Good coffee. You should have some."

The man was maddening. Aggravating.

Hot. Sexy.

Dressed in designer slacks and an open necked shirt with a gold chain around his neck, he exuded a casual confidence.

Deceptive. The thought criss-crossed her mind, and a sound, almost a snort tickled her throat, and she gulped it down. Beneath his casual air coiled the strength and power of a puma which, once unleashed, tore up everything in its path. His unquenchable drive fueled him to succeed in everything he did.

In everything except their marriage.

The snort blasted from her then, and although she slapped her hand over her mouth to muffle the sound, it tainted the air between them.

He quirked a brow, and she lowered her lashes a fraction, glancing at his rolled up sleeves.

His forearms were smattered with dark hair, and his hands invoked memories—him holding her, touching her in her most intimate places, loving her. Erotic sensations frisked her body, and she crunched the feelings she'd just as soon forget between her teeth.

"I removed your shoes and outer clothing—made you more comfortable."

"How thoughtful," she said, her words dripping with sarcasm, her toes curling on the tile. Compared to him she looked and sounded like a shrew, and that compounded her resentment against him.

"I can be."

"Where did you sleep?"

"Why, next to you."

"No."

"Mmm, yes."

28

She wanted to smack the 'gotcha' look off his face, but instead, she leaned against the balustrade and gripped the twisted metal rods between her fingers. Jasmine leaves brushed her skin, and the white star-shaped flowers filled the air with exotic scent.

"Can't have the help gossiping, now can we?"

"That never worried you before."

His eyes glittered, his shoulders tensed. "Indeed."

The early morning sun warmed her back, and she turned, her gaze skimming over the bougainvillea in the garden below, the scarlet blooms a contrast to the whitewashed villa. Lifting her lashes, she looked far out to sea at the sailboats dotting the horizon, and her thoughts went into reverse.

The flight from Paris to Athens had been anything but cordial. Taciturn, Michalis had sat next to her, his gaze glued on the sleeping child in her arms; but when he shifted his eyes to her, his tender look became eclipsed by the hardening of his pupils. A rip of dread pierced her, and she'd clutched Amy closer to her heart.

"Don't look at me like that," she'd said between her teeth.

"Like what?"

"Like I've committed some great sin."

He scratched his cheek with the pad of his thumb. "Conscience nipping at you?"

"No," she hissed. "It's not my conscience that's guilty, it's—"

"You'd better get some rest." He'd hauled himself up, reached for his laptop from the overhead compartment and settled on the seat across the aisle.

Several hours later, the Leonadis jet taxied to a stop on the runway of Athens International Airport, and Julia still refused to relinquish the child in her arms. Not during the drive to the villa, and not even after the chauffeur had set their suitcases in the foyer, and she and Michalis stood alone in the huge house.

"Let me help you with her." Michalis had reached for the baby, but she twisted away and climbed the stairs. "The nursery's on the right, adjacent to our bedroom."

She faltered in her step, but kept going, shutting her mind to everything and everyone. Especially Michalis, and his 'our bedroom' announcement. A maid appeared in the hallway, opening the nursery door and Julia stepped inside, hugging her daughter even tighter.

The nursery was a child's dream. A rainbow mural decorated one wall, teddy bear mobiles hung from the ceiling and stuffed toys were everywhere. The baby crib made of the finest polished wood and painted with cartoons, had the softest linen, and no doubt the most expensive.

A snicker trickled from her mouth. Michalis had given Amy everything in one day that money could buy ... everything Julia hadn't been able to give her in a year and might never be able to do.

Michalis wouldn't spare any expense for what, or whom, he considered belonged to him. And he'd laid claim to her and her baby for the next month. Her chest grew tight. Would she have to forfeit her child to Michalis at the month's end?

The query taunted her mind, sending a ripple of panic through her. She couldn't compete with the Leonadis' wealth. An explosion of air from her mouth, and the maid shot her a puzzled look. Julia gave her a brief smile, and swallowing emotion bruising her insides, laid her daughter on the fluffy mattress. Drawing the light blanket over her shoulders, she bent over and pressed her lips to the child's brow.

"I'll have your bags unpacked *Kyria*—"

"Thank you." Julia bypassed her into the adjoining bedroom. "But that can wait." As soon as the door closed behind her, she'd crashed out on the king-sized bed, squeezing the pillow in her arms. A tear had oozed between her lashes, then another ...

"I've hired a nanny," Michalis announced, his words echoing on the sunlit veranda and rocking Julia from her thoughts.

"What?"

"By tonight, you'll be fully rested," he said, his meaning unmistakable. "And to ensure you stay that way, I've hired a nanny for our daughter."

"No way."

"Yes." Michalis lifted the demitasse to his mouth and took another sip of the Greek brew, fixing her with a piercing look over the rim. "It'll ensure we won't be disturbed—"

"Michalis, I don't want my daughter looked after by a nanny. I'm perfectly capable—" She tossed him a cool glance over her shoulder, keeping her voice light but beneath her fingers, the steel design of the railing embedded in her palms. "There's no need."

"There is." He slammed the cup down and twisted in his chair, the sunlight glinting on his hair. Even as her mind rejected, another emotion prodded her to reach out, brush back the stray lock from his forehead … craving to touch him.

A seagull squawked, snapping her from her foolishness and reminding her why she was here and what she stood to lose.

"Why?"

He blotted the corner of his mouth with a napkin, his laser-sharp focus sending a clear signal.

"What's the rush?" she asked, her words a croak. Behind her, the surf crashed upon the sand, beckoning her back to the spectacular view of sea and sky curving around for miles.

"I want to get my month's worth of entertainment." He grinned … his mouth became a devilish slash, and she shifted away, the morning breeze cooling her hot cheeks. "And I want you to be in top form."

"That is so crass."

"In whose mind?"

She whipped around, about to hurl a blue streak at him, but at the last second, checked the impulse. Ignoring her twittering nerves, she took a deep breath and delivered him a more provocative response. "You hired me for the month … so … twenty-nine days left now."

"Keeping tabs already?"

31

Dismissing his mocking tone, she flicked her head back, flexed her fingers away from the steel bars and imagined she was working the catwalk as she sashayed toward him. "Why wait for tonight?"

"*Theos mou!*" He vaulted from the chair, a muscle boxing his jaw, a storm brewing in his eyes and the napkin squashed in his fist.

But Julia wouldn't leave well enough alone. For some perverse reason, she wanted to goad him to his limit, so she reached out, stroking his cheek with the tip of her finger. "I know how to *entertain* you."

"Had more practice, have you?"

A stunned silence, and then the crack of her hand across his cheek reverberated around them. She didn't know who was more shocked out of the two of them.

The stillness between them turned to a deadly calm, broken only by the ocean's mysterious concerto behind them.

"Get something to eat," he said, his words smooth steel, icy. Then, the corner of his mouth lifted … a leer if she ever saw one. "Once we get started, babe …" He brushed his cheek with the back of his hand, the imprint of her fingers stark upon his skin.

"I'm—" she began, but his next words jabbed and the apology dissolved on her tongue.

"We may not want to come up for air, let alone food."

All she could do was gape at him … gape at this remote stranger and wonder where she'd gone wrong. Had she ever known the man she married? She doubted it.

"We set sail at noon." He hurled the napkin on the table. "Be prompt."

"What's happened to you getting to know Amy?" She couldn't resist a jab of her own nor a lift of her brow.

"I intend to, but first—" He took a step closer and cupped her chin in his palm, his coffee-laced breath tickling her cheek, her mouth, and his thumb stroking her bottom lip. "I want to get reacquainted with you."

Julia swatted his hand away, and he laughed, the sound frosting her skin.

"I won't be separated from my baby."

"Amy will be in good hands." His suggestive look implied that Julia would also be in good hands—his. "We'll be back in a couple of days."

"I won't leave her with a stranger."

"Nor would I," he agreed, surprising her.

"I believe you've met the nanny once." His eyes glinted like ocean agates, drilling into her.

Julia shook her head, crinkling her brow. "I don't recall—"

"My meeting in Athens should only take a couple of hours." He nixed her words, glanced at the Omega watch on his wrist and strode toward the exit. "Don't be late."

"Very well," she sighed. "Amy and I will be ready."

He paused in stride. "Maria will take care of Amy."

A chill darted through her even though sunlight beat down upon her. "Maria?"

"The nanny."

She brushed her hands over her arms, banishing the unsettling premonition.

"You'll ... like her." He descended the stairs, his words mingling with the echo of his footsteps, and she couldn't be sure she'd heard right.

"What can I get for you, *Kyria*—"

Julia waved the maid away and plunked onto the chair, her heart thudding in her chest. Bypassing the heartier fare of cereal, milk, eggs and bacon, she snatched up a piece of toast.

The front door slammed shut, and she jumped, then the rev of the car motor ripped through the air making her grind her teeth in annoyance until the sound became muted in the distance.

"Grr!" She bit into the dry bread, imagining it was a piece of

Michalis' anatomy she'd sunk her teeth into. Thoughtfully she chewed, choked down the morsel, and knew she'd have to find a way to trump her soon to be ex-husband's plans.

Chapter 5

"Hey lighten up, you might enjoy spending the weekend with me." Michalis peered at her over his sunglasses and swerved the red coupé into his reserved parking space at Piraeus Harbor.

"I won't."

He tapped the steering wheel with his open palm and about to say something more, changed his mind and switched off the ignition. Jumping out, he swung around to her side, but she preempted him by opening the door and hopping out.

"Okay." He pinched the bridge of his nose, twisted around and swatted the fender with his hand. The tug-o-war between Julia and him had been percolating since this morning, and detonate it would. Until then, he intended to enjoy the thrill of battling and conquering the beauty queen standing before him with such icy disdain. "But I will enjoy the weekend."

Her sharp intake of breath nicked the silence between them. He studied her stiff back, her shapely derrière encapsulated in her short shorts, her tanned legs, trim ankles and feet strapped in flimsy sandals.

A sigh pulled its way from deep in his throat, and sounding more like a growl, he ground it down. Like the mythical Menelaus had launched a thousand ships to reclaim Helen of Troy, he'd been prepared to do the same to find Julia. His Adam's apple bounced, and the low rumble began building in his chest. Since then, the playing field had changed. He tightened his abs and the growl blasted from him in a cruel hush. Julia had not only deceived him by hiding his daughter, but had also spurned him. Her brittle words had raked across the iron shield he'd erected around his heart, but he'd felt the shockwaves of her contempt nonetheless.

"I'll … uh … get our bags." He back-stepped a few paces, tossed the car keys in the air and caught them smack in his palm.

"Whatever." She flicked a wisp of hair flirting on her mouth and stared out to sea.

He scrubbed a hand over his face, asphyxiating the words between his fingers. "This is not going well."

Julia remained a mystery, but the unveiling might prove an adventure, and thawing the ice-model an unexpected delight. His mouth twitched. Exactly what he'd thought when he first caught sight of her strolling the oceanfront boardwalk market nearly a year and a half ago after her photo shoot at the Acropolis. He stroked his chin with the car key. He'd gone further than a mere conquest then, and bound her to him in matrimony. She'd pulled a major stunt by ditching him—especially before he'd had a chance to explain—and definitely, it was time for a payoff.

"What'd you say?" She spun around, miffed.

"You got another pair of shoes?" He unlocked the hood, hauled out their duffle bags, and then banged it shut.

"Do I need them?"

"You might." Pocketing the car keys, he adjusted his sunglasses, and set his mouth in a straight line. He'd caught her, but look what it had gotten him … cost him. She'd snared him with her beauty, her virtue, her wiles, and then disappeared, taking with her a bigger prize than the Leonadis fortune.

His child.

His gut coiled, and his chest tightened. Never again would he fall for her seductive spell, her coquettish ways, and her velvet tongue. A grunt staggered upward from his belly and near exploded from his mouth.

She snapped her head up from tying the laces at her cleavage, and lifted a shapely brow.

"Need help with the tie?" He challenged her query with his raised eyebrow, and then slammed it level over his eye.

"No thank you." She stepped back, her mouth half open like she was about to spit venom his way, then sealed her lips.

"Anything breakable in here?" He indicated her bag, his tone rougher than he intended.

"No."

Against the backdrop of sea and sky, she stood tall and leggy in her white shorts, her skimpy top playing peek-a-boo with her midriff, the laced neckline dipping to the swell of her breasts. Red-hot memories taunted him, and he crushed them beneath his savage thoughts. Having to bargain for his child soured his tongue, scoured his belly, and blew his mind. His body though never missed a beat, primed and ready for her.

He tossed one bag over his shoulder and gripped the other in his fist, squashing the erotic kick in his gut.

Sunglasses shielded her eyes and a visor-cap shadowed her features, keeping her ponytail in place. The sea breeze tossed loose tendrils across her face, and he wanted to wrap the fickle curls around his index finger, cup her cheek and feel the silky smoothness of her skin.

His lungs inflated with air, and he clamped his teeth tight, exhaling through his nose.

Julia Armstrong Leonadis. Her name linked with his, booted up his temperature and sexual drive for this woman he'd made his wife for a brief time. This fashion model that was a combination of contrasts ... mystery and innocence ... fire and ice.

A scowl bit into his features.

Tonight he'd turn up the heat and melt the icecap sheathing her, and ensure an inferno blazed between them. A cruel twist marred his mouth. He'd take his due, secure what belonged to him and cast this hot deceptive babe adrift by the month's end.

"This way." He inclined his head toward the luxury yacht with the Leonadis Cruise Line logo and *Lady One* emblazoned across the bow. "The weekend will zip by soon enough."

"Not quickly enough for me." She marched past him across the dock, paused at the ramp and tapped her foot, her scarlet polished nails peeking from her roped sandals.

Chuckling, he stepped up behind her, so near his hips brushed her buttocks, and bending his head, he skimmed his mouth across her ear. "You might change your mind."

"I wouldn't bet on it," she snapped, jumping aside. She pushed her hands in the back pockets of her shorts, and stretched the cotton material of her cropped top across her breasts, unknowingly belting him with an erotic jolt smack center.

"Too bad." He walked the gangplank, tossed the bags on deck and hopped aboard the cruiser. "Come." She stepped onto the gangway, and when she drew closer, he extended a hand to help her onboard. "Watch your step."

"I'm fine." She twisted away, but the momentum bumped her off balance and clutching air, she headed for a dive in the ocean. "Oh noooo!"

An expletive exploded from Michalis' mouth, and he vaulted for her; the impact knocked him off axis, and he leaned backward boatside, landing on coils of rope and safety gear, his body cushioning her against the brunt of impact.

"Oomph!" he said, his aviators shooting off his nose.

"Oomph!" she said, her sunglasses flying into the air.

"I got you." He tightened his arms around her, and she jostled against him, her cheek pressed to his, her lips brushing the corner of his mouth.

Instantly she pulled back, her eyes colliding with his, her mouth parted, her breath grazing his lips. Her perfume, moist sunshine and roses stimulated, and he yanked her back into his embrace; her breasts crushing against his chest, her pelvis chaffing his hips, spiking his male counterparts on full alert.

A kick of emotion … er lust speared his gut, and he saw it reflected in her gaze.

"Julia …"

"Michalis …"

An ocean liner far out at sea blew its horn, the hollow sound penetrating through the haze of passion.

Julia fluttered her eyelashes, and seeming to come to her senses, struggled in his arms. "Let go."

A fueled moment, his libido warring with common sense, and then abruptly, he opened his arms. "Okay."

Just for a split second, confusion glazed her face, and tottering on his chest, she rolled over onto the deck. He leaped up, reached down and grabbing her elbow, hauled her to her feet. "Anything else?"

"No … yes … plenty." She shoved him back, the strap of her top sliding off her shoulder and revealing a vision of cleavage.

"Go for it," he muttered, the subtle innuendo flaring between them. Tensing his abs, his gaze bumped from her breasts to her posterior then glided down the length of her tanned legs, to her roped feet. A toe-ring gleamed on one of her toes, and he shook his head, amazed.

"I intend to." She adjusted her strap and swept past him, glancing around for her shades.

"Missed your chance," he said, a gust of wind whipping his hair. "It'll have to wait 'til we get to the hotel." What else would he find when he undressed her? A pierced belly button? A tattoo? Sweet sensation whacked his gut at the thought of suckling that part of her anatomy before nibbling his way lower to—

"Where might that be?"

He swept up her sunglasses, sauntered closer and hooked them on the neckline of her top, his fingers brushing the swell of her breast. She sucked in a whoosh of air. Pleased, he grinned and propped his shades on his nose.

"The Mermaid's—"

She paled, batting her lashes.

Was that a sheen of moisture or a glint of sunlight in her eye? He shrugged and chose the latter, easing the nick to his conscience.

"You wouldn't …"

"I did."

She hooked a stray curl behind her ear and set her sunglasses on her nose. "You have a bizarre sense of humor." Was her voice just a little strained?

"If you say so," he ground out, his words barely audible. Swiping his finger around the collar of his tennis shirt, he noted the perspiration glazing her upper lip. "Would you … if you'd like a drink, there's some in the fridge down below."

"I know where they are." Julia skirted a wide girth around him, back-stepping all the way. "I remember."

"Then you must also remember—"

"I'd rather not," she bit back, crunching down the lure into the past. Every image, touch, kiss … every nuance of their honeymoon night had been seared into her heart.

The prelude had begun on the yacht beneath the stars, spot-lighted by the moon and serenaded by the ocean. It had been heaven. Later, at the enchanted Mermaid's Grotto, a seduction of the senses combusted to the tempo of their heartbeats, and even the sea-foam washing over them hadn't dampened a degree of their fervor.

She'd clung to him; her husband, her lover, her guy, until she thought she'd die from the exquisite torture in his arms.

"No." It had been a million years ago … She'd been a carefree, laughing girl with the world at her feet and Prince Charming at her side. Her lips twisted in contempt. He'd morphed into the big bad ogre.

40

"Not thirsty?" Michalis heaved equipment aside and checked the safety gear. "You mind bringing me up a beer?"

She snapped her teeth together, her response garbled, but he continued working, his back to her. His shoulder blades contracted, a sweat stain already dampening the t-shirt now drawn taut across his back, his biceps bulging with each heave-ho of the rigging.

A tremor rocked her senses, and she slammed her fist to her mouth, smothering the bleat of sound. Not long ago, she'd thought she couldn't breathe … function without him; never imagined leaving … leaving him.

Until that traitorous day … Bitterness stung her tongue, and she curled her hands, her fingernails biting into her palms.

But she had left with her pride in tatters, and harboring a secret.

Somehow, she had continued to breathe—one breath at a time … for her baby.

Images of all she'd, no, they'd had and lost branded her brain cells and tears blurred her vision. A repeat performance she couldn't allow; wouldn't stand. She batted her eyelashes behind her sunglasses, staying a sob with a swift suction of oxygen and almost keeled over. She lunged for the life preserver tacked to the wall, keeping herself upright, but still shaken.

The sob managed to work its way into her throat but she muffled the sound with the back of her hand. His cold and calculating agenda rattled her insides. What interest could he have in Amy, except as the carrier of the Leonadis bloodline? Julia narrowed her eyes, determined to navigate the month without any emotional bruises and no losses. Then, "*Yasoo*, Michalis," the words a hush of sound between her fingers.

"Is that a yes to the beer?" He tossed a coil of rope in the lazerette, the stern storage area and barely glanced her way.

"More orders, Cap'n?" She spun around, and the tensing of his shoulders cued he hadn't missed her sarcastic tone. Going on the offensive, she slapped him with a flippant remark. "Where's the crew?"

"We're it." He shot her a lopsided grin, and dang it, it still made her heart rate go into overdrive. And just because of that, there was an added edginess to her voice.

"You're taking a lot for granted."

"Am I?" He straightened to his six-foot height and studied her head to toe, sending prickles of awareness through her. "Figured you could handle first mate basics."

"Not sure I remember how," she murmured.

"I'll help—"

"No."

He probed her features with his shadowed gaze, dipped to her breasts, then lower at the apex of her thighs. A sweep of the length of her legs to her feet, then his lazy gaze eased its way back up her curves to her face and settled on her mouth.

She licked her lips.

He drew in a forced breath.

Every spot he'd branded her with his hot gaze, sizzled, and it had nothing to do with the sun beating down upon them. But she had to be strong and not give in to his magnetism, his sexuality, his—charisma.

"Don't provoke me, Michalis." She spun away, her words no defense against the tsunami of sensation washing over her. He'd always been able to turn her on with one look, one touch … her breath jammed in her chest … one kiss.

His sexy smile.

But although her body thrummed to a tempo of the senses, her mind stayed resolute, denying the attraction, her heart sealed behind a wall of indifference.

"And why not?" He came up behind her, the silent tread of his Nikes not giving her any warning, and encircled her waist, his mouth nuzzling her nape. A rush of air filled her lungs, and she allowed it to ease between her teeth, her pulse leaping out of sync.

She could not, must not have any feelings … feelings of the finer sort for him. This stranger she'd married had destroyed her a year ago and now was about to fell her a second time using their daughter as ammo.

A flick of his tongue behind her earlobe, then a puff of his breath sensitized her nerve endings. She could so easily lean back into him, reach up and slide her fingers in his hair, turn in his arms, lift her face to his, feel his mouth on hers—

She clenched her hands, girding her resolve not to succumb to his sensuality and jerked away, eliminating the friction of his powerful legs against hers, the hair chafing her bare thighs, another stimulant of his male potency.

A hiss between his teeth, his probing gaze pinning her to the deck, his hands still on her shoulders.

"I-I'm going down below," she blurted, the words a gasp of sound.

"We set sail in five. Be ready."

She propped her sunglasses on her visor and favored him with a cool look. "Aye, aye, Cap'n." Flouncing past him, she scrambled down the stairs to the galley, the echo of his chuckle drifting down to her and making her skin bounce with goose bumps.

She rubbed her arms with her hands, and avoiding the adjacent sleep-quarters, paused in the middle of the cabin. "Steady, girl." Since the air conditioning hadn't kicked in yet, it was stuffy, and brushing her moist palms on her backside, she made a beeline for the icebox. Yanking the door open, she grabbed a can of Pepsi, flipped it open and swallowed several mouthfuls. The fizz tickled her nose and the caffeine gave her a nice little buzz.

"Hits the spot every time." She grinned, and cradling the can between her palms, peered out the porthole at the myriad of power watercraft docked along the wharf. Frowning, she pursed her lips and her cheeks dimpled. She should be able to handle Michalis for a few days, until she secured the trust deed for Amy.

After all, she worked the catwalk with a bat of an eyelash, a sway of her hips, a tilt of her head.

How hard could it be with Michalis? She stomped across the floor and plunked down on the plush sofa, propping her feet on the coffee-table. Rolling the can across her forehead, she slid it down her temples to her throat and brought it to rest at her cleavage, the condensation cooling her hot skin. She wasn't good at subterfuge … detested it in fact.

Subterfuge, or the art of deception for gain, her stripper mother had once explained, made men empty their wallets and drop their pants; then at their most vulnerable, she'd cash out. By next morning, her mother had packed them up and bussed them into another town, a new strip joint and another sucker.

An anguished sound burst from Julia's mouth, and she closed her eyes. Eventually, the FBI had caught her mother, locked her in the slammer and assigned Julia to a foster home. Somehow, her mother had managed to beat the rap.

A quick phone call telling Julia she'd be back for her after trying her luck overseas, had been an empty promise. Julia shouldn't have been surprised, but at eleven, she'd felt abandoned, unwanted … unloved.

Raising the can to her lips, Julia took another sip, the fizz of liquid quenching her thirst and easing the lump in her throat. She'd never seen her mother again. The only memento, a mangled photo of them she'd kept in her wallet.

Julia batted the sting from her eyes. She wanted better for her and Amy … a home, a sweet place to call home.

A sigh wrenched from her mouth, and she scanned the room, backtracked, and squinted at a photo propped upon the shelf beneath the porthole. A frown, a blink, then a series of blinks, and she banged the can on the table, cola sloshing over the top. She scrambled up and seized the picture in a two-handed choke-hold.

A happy home with Michalis was not in the cards. A tremor

of seismic proportions shook her every cell, but she forced herself to look, lest she forget, lest she be lulled into a false sense of security.

"Once a cad, always a louse." The words snapped off her tongue and tainted the air with resentment.

In the photo, the dark-haired young woman leaned into him, her mouth pressed to his cheek and her eyes sparkling. Michalis looked down at her with indulgence, a protective arm slung around her shoulders. Julia swayed, the memories pummeling her mind.

The picture blurred.

A forced breath erupted from her, and she fluttered her lashes to clear her vision. In the photo, another man stood in the shadowed doorway of the seaside Cabaret with the flashing neon sign.

"No doubt his security turning a blind eye to the tryst," Julia hiccupped, her chest tightening. Her eyes fixated on the damning words, *'Efharisto,* you've changed my life! *M'agape,* M.'

Thank you and my love. Julia understood the basic Greek words that slayed her.

Julia smacked the photo back on the shelf and gripped the edge. Blackness danced before her, and sucking in life-giving oxygen, exhaled in a burst of passion, trying to regain her composure.

"Awfully quiet down there." Michalis' deep voice drifted to her from above but that only spiked her ire.

She glared out the porthole at the horizon, the sea a golden hue with flecks of sun-fire, and rubbed tension from her nape with quivery fingers. The sound of a motor launch setting out to sea fractured her thoughts, and a stiff smile cracked her mouth. She turned away to get his beer from the fridge, her smile turning to a chuckle, and then a high-pitched laugh, stripping gloss from the teak cabin walls.

"Hey, you okay?" he hollered down the stairwell, his footsteps echoing above her.

"Uh … yeah," she murmured, then added a lilt to her voice. "Yep, be right up."

She heard him marching to the helm station to take the wheel, and then, "Anchors away!"

A second later, the motor revved and the boat lurched forward, sending Julia lunging for the sofa to keep her bearings. Once the rhythm of the engine hit its groove, she found her sea legs and paced the confines of the cabin. She choked the bottleneck in her hand and cast the picture a last cursory glance. Definitely, she'd have to find a way to best the big 'n mighty Michalis Leonadis.

But she'd not do it with her stinging tongue and cold shoulder.

She twisted the top off the bottle, took a refreshing swallow of beer, and then trashed it. Another soft drink was a safer bet. She had to be focused, sharp. Her mother had left her with a few gems of wisdom when it came to the opposite sex, if she dared use them. She squashed the warning from her mind and thought of Amy's future.

Crinkling her brow, she caught her bottom lip between her teeth. She'd disarm the wealthy magnate with the art of seduction—a sour taste tinged her tongue, but she paid it no heed. Charm, honeyed words, womanly wiles … her sexuality. And when he least expected it, whammo!

What if it backfired? The rapid tempo beat in her brain, but she rejected the signal for caution.

Once Amy's inheritance was secure, she'd take her baby and bolt; Michalis could hire the Trojan army to come after her for all she cared.

Score even!

Chapter 6

"Michalis *mou*." Julia gritted her teeth, pinned a smile on her face and forced the words out. "Would you like some *mezethakia?*" She held out the tray of snacks and an ice-cold Athenian beer.

"What's this now?" He shot her a tentative glance and resumed navigation. "Greeks bearing gifts?"

"Gifts, yes." She favored him with her dimpled cheek, but he didn't catch it, his attention on the ocean. "Greek, no."

"A mere technicality." He twirled the wheel in his hands, his gaze straying back to her. "You married a Greek."

A silent beat, broken only by the rush of waves against the bow slicing through the water.

"Should I be on guard, Julia?" he mocked, seizing the bottle of beer.

She averted her gaze, set the tray on the stool and grabbed onto the doorframe to steady her legs. "Perhaps it is I who must be on alert."

"Perhaps." He tilted the bottle to his mouth, took a swig and smacked his lips in appreciation, underscoring his devil may care attitude.

That one word delivered in such a casual tone, almost too cavalier, sent a frisson of unease through her. Abruptly, she turned her back to him, staring out to sea; the rhythm of the boat slicing through the water calmed her nerves, and she almost laughed at her foolish imaginings. So much so, that for the next couple of hours she actually enjoyed the ocean excursion.

Soon after, the windmills overlooking Mykonos town came into view to the backdrop of whitewashed buildings scaling the mountainside. Julia blew out a breath, awed by the beauty of Mykonos, the Jewel of the Aegean.

"A quick stop to refuel and—"

"No tour here?" She turned halfway toward him, ignoring the pang of regret stabbing her heart. The place held so many memories for her … her and Michalis; before he so callously stripped happiness from her life.

"No time." He drained the bottle of beer, set it on the tray and popped a stuffed grape-leaf in his mouth, chewed, swallowed. "Mmm, good. Your culinary skills have improved."

"Nope." She'd never been much good at cooking, and certainly had no chance to practice her hand during the short span of their marriage; the resident housekeeper and staff had taken care of all their domestic needs. "Frozen microwavable packs."

But what she'd lacked in the kitchen, she more than made up in the bedroom, he'd often murmured in her ear in their most intimate moments. The mere recollection had her blushing, and grasping the tray, she spun around to return below, the heat from her cheeks spreading through her body.

"Tasty nonetheless."

Julia paused in her tracks, and thinking his snappy retort held a hidden meaning, tossed him a narrowed gaze. But he'd already dismissed her, concentrating on docking the super-sized cruiser alongside the quay. Fine by her. The less interaction she had with Michalis Leonadis the better.

"A quick stop at the office to check a few things and we'll be cruising again."

Her jaw nearly dropped, together with the tray in her hands.

Michalis was actually clueing her into his schedule? She pressed the edge of the tray against her abdomen and muffled a chuckle. But he heard and speared her with his hard gaze.

"You never could separate business from play." As soon as the words left her mouth, she bit her tongue, but quick on the uptake, he nailed her.

"Not to worry—"

"I'm not—"

"Once we get started with … er … play, you'll have my undivided attention."

"No, thanks."

His laughter sailed over her, sparking both her desire and fury.

"We'll see, *yeneka mou*."

Her stomach plummeted, then righted. The last surprise … er … shock she'd gotten from the great Leonadis, had detonated her world, leaving her in a heap of rubble. Only the thought of her baby had kept her going step-by-step, moment-by-moment, and day-by-day. And her friend, Nina, having gone through her own woes with her Manhattan millionaire, had taken Julia in until she'd been able to get to Paris. A misty smile brushed her lips. After the baby was born, Chachee had come to the rescue with a job offer.

A sigh ruffled from deep within her. She was glad Nina and Cade had worked things out and were happy. But for her and Michalis there'd be no happily ever after, not after what he'd done, then ruthlessly dared use their daughter as a gaming chip. Heartless boor. As soon as the month was over, she'd skip out with Amy—

Her turbulent thoughts skidded to a stop, and her breath lodged in her chest. Isn't that what her mother had done? Her hands shook, and the bottles on the tray rattled, finally tipping over. How far could she run from Michalis? And for how long?

"Something wrong?" He tossed her a glance over his shoulder, and then focused on docking the yacht along the quay.

"I can do without surprises," she murmured but her words carried in the breeze.

"I'm with you there," he muttered, his features harsh in the sunlight.

"Red-letter day," she batted back, the banter somehow accentuating the weightier matter beneath. "We agree on something,"

"Do we, Julia?" He tightened his hands on the wheel, his mouth set.

"Is that a rhetorical question, or do you want an answer?" she challenged him.

"It's not, and I do." He met and held her gaze, tapped the wheel and changed the subject. "This shouldn't take more than an hour. We should be at the resort by late afternoon."

"Don't rush your meeting on my account."

He chuckled at her ploy to delay the inevitable. "It'll be an evening to remember."

"I can wait."

He laughed harder, and she stomped her way down below, shutting out his amusement at her expense.

"Mario, meet my ... er ... wife." Michalis turned to the young man leaning against the convertible near the waterfront taxi station, then back to her.

"Julia, this is Mario Alexos, my second in command and the best legal mind in the country."

That had her radar on alert, but she smiled at the 'best legal mind' as he ushered her into the back of the Porsche. Michalis slid into the front seat.

"I've dispensed with the formalities of the limo, today," Mario confessed. "It's too nice a day not to have a run with the wind blowing through our hair, the smell of the ocean, the—"

Michalis guffawed and rubbed the back of his neck. "Did I just call you my second in command?"

"Sure thing, boss." Mario grinned, jumping into the driver's seat and turning on the ignition.

During the short drive to the satellite office of the Leonadis International Cruise Line, the men carried on a conversation, and Julia creased her forehead deep in thought.

Mario seemed to be another typical Greek heartbreaker, but something about him teased her memory. Unable to place him, she dismissed the annoying niggle, reclined on the expensive upholstery and let the fresh island air whip her hair in her face.

When Mario screeched to a stop in front of the modern office building, a rare find on the island, Michalis twisted in his seat, his arm stretching across the upholstery. "Can you amuse yourself for an hour?"

"Sure can." She scrambled out, thanking Mario for opening the door for her as her gaze fell on the waterfront market, abuzz with activity.

Michalis followed her line of vision. "I'll meet you at the Seaside Taverna."

"Okay, but first I'd like to make a phone call."

Except for her wallet stuffed in the pocket of her shorts, she'd left her gear, including her cell phone on the boat. So she had no other recourse but to walk beside Michalis through the double glass doors, across the foyer and into his private office on the second floor overlooking the harbor.

When the two men stepped into the conference room, Julia grabbed the phone and keyed in the babysitter's number. She heard Amy gurgling in the background, and it warmed her heart and brought a smile to her face.

Before they'd left, true to his word, Michalis had escorted her next door to the babysitter's and she'd made a beeline for her daughter in the backyard. But, Amy enamored with a stuffed panda in the bouncy chair beneath a gnarled olive tree hadn't even noticed her.

"Already got a mind of your own, munchkin." Julia had bent down and kissed her cheek.

"Like her mother." Michalis had murmured in her ear, sending her thoughts into a tailspin and tingles dilating through her.

Before she could slap him with an icy retort, he'd introduced her to the nanny. Dressed in denim shorts and a cropped t-shirt, she lounged on a garden chair, sunglasses and a sunhat keeping her face in shadow. Reluctantly, the girl turned from watching Amy and peered at Julia over the rim of her shades.

After she and Julia had exchanged a few words, Michalis had spoken in rapid-fire Greek with the girl that Julia couldn't follow what they said.

The nanny smiled and placing her hand on his forearm, murmured something for his ears alone. For some uncanny reason, Julia wanted to rip the other woman's arm off. Ridiculous of course, since she didn't give a fig what Michalis did, right?

"*Kala.*" He patted her hand. "Good."

He'd had the gall to stroke the other woman's hand in front of her. Julia didn't know whether to spit or rush out affronted. In the end she did neither, and gulping down the acid on her tongue maintained her composure.

When he'd crouched down and caressed their daughter's hair with his fingers, the tenderness in his eyes tugged at Julia's heart; before she could make sense of her emotions, he'd leaped up, taken her elbow and guided her out.

"*Efharisto.*" Julia spoke her thanks into the mouthpiece and set the phone back on its cradle on the desk. Knowing her daughter was safe, she breathed a sigh of relief, but it was tempered with a pang of regret.

If only … she glanced at the door Michalis had walked through moments earlier, and splayed her palms on the desk. Strong, sleek, expensive, just like the man. Reminiscing on 'if only … ' belonged in La La Land, and this was the real world; the world in which she had to trump the ruthless man wheeling and dealing behind the half-closed door. She squeezed her hands closed, tempted to pound on the hardwood, but instead she flexed her fingers. The man who'd wield his power, his money and his connections to take her daughter from her ... and wouldn't even blink.

She stared out the wide expanse of window at the oceanfront buzzing with activity and rubbed her throbbing temples. Their hushed voices filtered through to her from behind the door, but unable to decipher their conversation, she crossed the floor to go down to the lobby, and stumbled.

"Everything ok, Julia?" Michalis' deep voice filtered through the half open door, but he remained behind it.

"Yes, thanks." Julia regained her step, her hand spanning the frosted glass partition separating them. "Amy's just—" But Michalis had resumed his legal strategy discussion with Mario. This time, some of their words sailed within earshot. "The American Lol ... claim ... deed ... no record except ..." A pause. "... her daughter ..." A chill ran through her. Was Amy's trust fund that Michalis had promised a sham? She flew down the stairs to the lobby and out the door, the heat a shocking contrast to the air-conditioned office.

But the sunlight soothed her frayed nerves, and she kept on walking.

She knew full well what was going down between Michalis and his second in command, the legal whiz. She licked her dry lips and meandered through the crowds, all the while thinking— she had to find a way to stop the shipping magnate who owned the world from taking her little part of it.

A pause in step, and a glimmer of hope flashed in her mind. But he didn't own her, or her daughter.

Not yet. The taunt batted back. *You're here aren't you?*

"Maybe I should bundle up Amy and ride out of Dodge." The words flittered from her mouth, then she chuckled at her whimsical notion.

Sure enough, Michalis would ride after her until he lassoed what he wanted.

Sunrays bouncing off the concrete hit her in the face, and adjusting her visor and sunglasses, she hurried to the seaside plaza abuzz with festivity. Date palms afforded shade to the vendors, but oblivious to the heat, tourists flashed cameras, lounged in outdoor cafés beneath colorful umbrellas, sipping ice-cold cocktails or Greek coffee and munching *baklava*; others laughing, bargained with the locals for souvenirs; silks, embroidered clothing, seashell knickknacks and a myriad of other crafts.

"A cool lemonade would go down well right about now," Julia thought out loud, missing this easygoing life she'd come to know. A quick glance about, and she grinned. She even missed the local pelican scavenging for tidbits at the wharf-side *kafenions*.

"No." It'd be foolhardy to think about the past. Focusing on getting through the next four weeks before she and Michalis parted company for good would be the smarter move. That optimistic thought put a bounce in her step, and she strolled along the quay bazaar for bargains.

After about an hour, she collapsed in a chair beneath a canopy of grape vines, set her shopping bag on the empty chair next to her and ordered a drink. Fanning her face with her hand, she listened to the *bouzouki* musicians and watched the Greek folk-dancers inviting tourists to join the circle in the shade of a giant carob tree.

"*Opa!*" someone shouted, followed by clapping to the beat.

A smile quivered on her mouth, and she sighed. It seemed so long ago that she'd been carefree and laughing … her mind now set on rewind …

After she'd wrapped an early photo shoot at the Acropolis for a line of Grecian-style *couture*, she'd stolen away for a couple of hours before she was due for wardrobe and makeup for a session at the Parthenon. She'd been like a kid in a candy store, immersed

54

in local color, flavor and the hospitality of the grinning shop-keepers.

She'd been bartering with a merchant over a bracelet, and knowing only a handful of Greek phrases, he seemed to be getting the upper hand; until tall, dark and sexy stepped in and with a few words, had the vendor agreeing to his smokin' deal.

Laughing, she made to pay for it, but Michalis had said, "Allow me." When she demurred, he hiked a brow, paid for it and slipped it on her wrist. A walk along the pier, some flirtatious banter, and he had her sitting at the Seaside Taverna sipping an iced coffee to the sounds of *bouzouki* and the surf.

It had been magical … that first day, the second and the third. And—

"*Kyria* Leonadis." The café owner now grinned beneath his mustache and set her drink with a sprig of mint on the table. "We're delighted you're back."

"It's good to be here." She rifled in her wallet for a euro, and realized she meant what she'd said.

The owner held up his hand. "On the house, *Kyria* Leonadis."

Julia smiled her thanks. The locals were almost like family in this small town … everybody knew everybody's business … well almost.

"I don't know how your husband does it."

At her puzzled look, he wiggled his bushy brows. "First, he got the prettiest girl" —he winked and had her laughing— "then, he lured my best waiter to law school and to his company."

"Yes, he has a knack at getting what he wants."

"So far a perfect record, *ne*?" He turned to go, his dark eyes merry and already waving to another customer.

Although his words were innocent, to Julia they held an ominous message. She couldn't allow Michalis to continue with his 'perfect record' where she and Amy were concerned.

To ease the unsettling feeling, Julia extracted several bills from her wallet, tossed the hefty tip on the table and settled back, tapping her foot to the tempo of the music and sipping her lemonade.

She got so carried away with the festivities, that by the time she glanced at her watch, the sun flamed the horizon and turned the sea to mystery. A string of lights looped from tree to tree blinked, the dancers had changed costumes, the band strumming the evening's serenade. Nightlife was a bomb with the Greeks— plenty of food, drink, company and merriment … *kefi*. Passion for life!

She grimaced, and pushed away her almost empty glass. She'd succumbed to the perpetual romance of the Greeks, and it had been to her detriment. Shaking herself from her despondent mood, she scanned the milling crowd and drummed her fingers on the table.

Where was Michalis? Unlike her, he was always punctual. A sliver of fear zinged through her, but she bashed it away. "Silly."

Shoving her chair back, she stood ready to walk back to the office and demand an explanation, when she caught sight of him weaving through the throng. She gripped the rough-hewn table edge, a hand fluttering to her throat and heat singeing her skin.

He stood head and shoulders above the rest, and with his purposeful stride he was fast approaching her table. Propping his shades on his head, he scanned the area, frowned, and when he saw her, tension eased from his features. It took him only seconds to bridge the distance between them, and shifting an attaché case from one hand to the other, he gripped her elbow. "Let's go."

She blinked, and stood her ground. "What? No, how was your day, dear, what'd you buy?" She held up the bag with a cute swimsuit in it for Amy.

"You can tell me on the way," he mused, guiding her through the revelers to the car.

"Where's Mario?"

"Locking in a Tokyo deal that blew up last ye—" He crunched down on his words, his jaw rigid. "He's working."

Ushering her into the passenger seat, he tossed his attaché on her lap and slid into the driver's seat. "He'll pick the car up later." He turned the key in the ignition, the motor revved, and they zoomed off. "For the next two days, I'm officially off." He swerved to bypass a horse and cart. "Except for the emergency transmitter onboard, no cell calls, no computers, no gadgets, no—"

"I don't believe it."

"Neither do I, but I'm game." He grinned. "No interruptions of any kind." His hot gaze slid over her, scalding her nerve endings. "I expect your undivided attention ... amongst other things."

"How will the nanny reach me ... us in an emergency?"

"She'll call Mario, and he'll radio in." And to emphasize his words, he pressed on the gas pedal and picked up speed. "Don't worry. In a real emergency, the Leonadis chopper will come to the rescue."

"All plotted out," she said, her words brittle.

"Not exactly as I'd frame it, but if you insist—" He set his mouth, the warning in his tone suspended in the air between them.

But she wouldn't let up. "I don't have to insist ... I know."

"Really?"

She batted his query, and imagined it skipping across the water. "Sure do."

"Enlighten me."

"Well ... uh ..." She'd be alone with him out at sea, then on the island resort miles from anywhere, and the jitters pounced. Feeling vulnerable, her emotions were already spiking, and her body hummed for him. To counter that realization, she fired back, and her bullet-sharp words found their mark. "You're a control freak, Michalis."

"What the heck is that supposed to mean?" He guffawed, but it was a dry sound.

About to hammer him back, she swiped her hand across her moist forehead, her tone softening a tad. "Michalis, what are we doing?"

"Going away for the weekend?"

The man was aggravating. "Be serious."

"I am."

"We'll end up hating each other more—"

He skidded into the parking spot, twisted the ignition off and swiveled in his seat, his eyes probing hers, his chin jutting. "Will that be a problem for you?"

"No," she blasted the word. "But it might be for Amy."

"Amy's not here, Julia."

"Precisely." She gripped the attaché case so hard her fingers hurt. "You don't want Amy—"

"Not want my child?"

"—for any other reason than to continue the Leonadis bloodline."

He paled, his features taut, but he didn't deny it. A humorless sound exploded from his mouth, sheathing her body with goosebumps. "And you Julia, how are you using our child?"

"I don't know what you're talking about."

"Well, here's my take." He stroked his chin and pursed his mouth. "You used me. And after you got the child ... the family you wanted, you snuck out of town."

"No," she blurted. "I left because—" She shook her head, and the rest of her explanation melted down her throat. He knew why she'd left.

"A father's not part of the equation?"

She blanched. "Of course, but—" The words fractured on her tongue, a shard of pain piercing her, and she gripped the doorhandle. She hadn't known her father, doubted her mother knew for sure; she wanted better for her daughter.

"To the Greeks there's nothing so important as family … a child."

That nicked her pride … her fury. "You forfeited that right when you and that—that bimbo—"

His features turned granite hard, his eyes glacial. "You were saying?"

"Never mind." She glanced around at the busy pier. "This is not the time to—"

"Perhaps you're right."

"Will there ever be a right time, Michalis?"

"At the end of the month." He leveled her with a shuttered gaze, a nerve battering his jaw. "That should tell the tale."

A suspended moment of disbelief, then she burst out laughing, otherwise she'd be screaming like a shrew. "Proves my point."

"Which is?"

"Controlling bast—"

"Tuh, tuh," he goaded. "A sailor's blue streak from your fair lips?"

She rolled her eyes heavenward, but before she fired back, he'd hopped out and this time beat her to opening the door.

"Come on, I want to sail before dusk."

"Why?"

He lifted a brow, and a lazy smile split his mouth.

Seductive. Enticing. Magnetic.

And she floundered like a fish on a hook … but she fought like her life depended on it.

It did.

"Because I want you bathed in the twilight, amidst the backdrop of the horizon, attending to my every need, want, desire."

She drew in a sharp breath, carving her throat. How could she have allowed herself to be lulled into a false sense of security? Michalis Leonadis was back at full force, tracking his original agenda.

Ruthless. Hard. Unyielding.

That's how he crushed his competition and anyone who crossed him.

And she'd crossed him, big time.

He'd make her pay for skipping out on him and costing him a fortune … she'd seen the headlines in Italia … *Bride ditches Greek shipping magnate, sinking billion dollar Tokyo deal.*

Shivers shimmied up her spine. She had to level the playing field to even remotely stand a chance of coming out of this unscathed. And as much as she loathed it, she had to play her ace on Michalis—her mom's tricks o' the trade.

"Tonight, and tomorrow night and the next and—"

"I'll give you more"—a dip of her lashes—"than you bargained for, Michalis *mou*." She reached up, stroking his cheek with her fingertips, and tried not to jolt from the electric volt charging into her. The man was fueled with testosterone to explosive levels, and if she missed a beat, she could end up totally fried emotionally.

"You don't say?" He flashed her a white-toothed smile, his gaze narrowed.

"Oh, but I do," she purred, and swallowed her uncertainty.

"Then, what are we waiting for?"

Chapter 7

"All aboard." Michalis waved her ahead of him and dissected her every movement beneath his dark brows.

"Here." Julia turned, shoving the attaché case at him with such force, he tottered on his heels, and she swept past him.

A chuckle scratched his throat but didn't sound. He could smell a con job a mile off. Had even done so as a youth, but his uncle had paid him no mind. Instead, in a drunken stupor he'd set sail with his floozy … er … love of his life, and never returned, leaving Michalis to care for the boats and his little sister.

Over the years, wheeling and dealing with the global sharks had sharpened his instincts to detect a snow job at its inception. His gaze followed Julia traipsing along the pier, the sway of her hips and the swing of her arms, a trigger to a fool's fantasies.

Julia was up to no good.

He'd slipped once where she was concerned and that rankled his pride. But he never made the same mistake twice, especially with a woman … he had no intention of being suckered a second time by Julia.

Suckered like his uncle—a fierce pressure built inside him— who'd transferred half the fledgling Leonadis boat business, now worth a fortune, to his American Loli—the pressure detonated from him. And she'd bequeathed it to her only relative—a daughter.

"Move along," he commanded, marching up behind her.

As soon as the weekend tryst with Julia wrapped, he'd get an update from Mario and nab Amy. She was no doubt a gold digger like her mother.

"Not so fast." Julia skidded to a stop, and he almost bumped into her shapely derriere.

Friction crackled in the inch of space separating them, and he dropped the attaché across his hips, camouflaging his body's reaction.

The woman still turned him on, and that had him clamping down on his molars. She was a major turn-on, but she didn't have to know that.

She spun around, hands on hips and jabbed her finger at his chest.

Sizzles zinged into him.

"I want to see the trust deed," she demanded, her voice wavering. A blink, and she averted her gaze.

Another ploy? He frowned.

"I want proof you'll keep your promise that Amy's future is secure."

He inflated his lungs, and a second later the air exploded from his mouth. "Right here." He tapped the attaché case, and she pounced for it, but he held it out of her reach. "Uh, uh."

"Why not?"

"You've got to uphold your end of the deal first."

"But how do I know if—"

"You don't." His cruel words surprised him almost as much as her. "There's something to be said for … trust."

She gaped at him, and then burst out laughing, the brittle sound lacerating his insides. And because of that, his next words were even more unyielding. "I'm going to lock this in the safe below, until we're square."

She gave him a glazed look, and nibbled her bottom lip.

He felt a prick of his conscience, but he crushed it before it took root.

"Got that, cover girl?"

A slight lowering of her lashes, and she ran her fingertip down his chest, his muscles tightening beneath her touch. "A look at the document, might make me more amiable to your overtures."

"Might do." He curled his lip. "But I don't intend to pay to play prematurely."

"Pay is pay, Michalis," she blasted, her words breaking on her tongue.

"Come now, Julia." He squinted at her, his tone laced with censure. "That's so cold, no?

"Got that one right, Michalis." She flung her head back and skirted a wide girth around him onto the boat.

Chuckling, he leaped on deck. "We'll just have to heat things up then, won't we?"

Oh, yeah. He'd ensure whatever surprises she might spring on him were pleasure bound, but it'd cost him. Patience. Caution. He'd have to exercise both where she was concerned until he felt vindicated. A self-deprecating grunt, and he watched her strolling to the deck chair. The problem was, he'd never been patient or cautious where she was concerned.

Shaking his head, he turned to vault the stairs to the safe below and an unexpected gust smacked him, hurling him back in time …

He was a kid of twelve racing down the beach, his toes sinking in the sand, the wind whipping through his hair and salt-tang stinging his cheeks.

Trying to outrace one of his uncle's boat rentals chug-a-lugging to shore, he slid to a stop, sending sand flying with his foot and howled with glee. He'd won, and plunged into the ocean, helping pull the skiff ashore …

Ocean spray moistened his face, and he blinked the past behind him, snaring Julia in his sights. Oh yeah, she was up to something. He curled his lip and heavy-stepped it across the deck to the helm station. The motor revved, and chuckling, he gripped the wheel, relishing the sheer power vibrating beneath his hands.

"What's funny?" She yanked off her visor and plunked down on a lounger.

"Settle in, Beautiful." He winked, pulling out of the harbor into the Aegean—an amalgamation of sea, sky and flaming sunset. "This won't take long."

Mist from the white-capped waves spritzed her face, and she sputtered at the saltiness on her lips.

Michalis laughed the harder, and smart man that he was uttered not a word, navigating northeast from Mykonos. Obviously miffed, she stretched out on the lounger and closed her eyes, ignoring him.

A sunbeam caught the gold in her hair, and he was tempted to abandon the wheel and vault to her side, burying his face in her curls and breathing her scent laced with ocean mist.

The wheel throbbed beneath his hands.

A modern goddess; perfect from the top of her head to her scarlet tipped toes. Her skin glistened in the waning sunlight, her hair glimmered and the swell of her breasts glowed.

He eased his grip on the wheel, his fingers stroking the smoothness of wood. A low rumble rapped his rib cage. He remembered how he'd cherished her with his hands, his mouth, and his body.

"No." The denial scorched off his tongue, yet the ache tore through him. He must not feel a thing for her, the deserter. The deceiver. He twisted his mouth in contempt. She'd dissed him without a hearing and pronounced him guilty outright.

Her scorn had knocked him for a loop, making him feel a bigger fool than his uncle had, when he'd been duped by his American Lolita. His gut coiled, fueling him with ice-cold fury to turbo-charge his M.O. for retribution. No way in hell was he hitting the skids like his uncle had over a woman.

You've already been had, big guy. The taunt stabbed his mind. *She's cost you more than cash.* Stone-faced, he twirled the wheel beneath his hands and rode roughshod over the waves. "Shut up," he muttered, but the wind carried his words.

"What'd you say?" She lifted an eyelash, her tone detached, and that irked him no end.

"Nothing," he said, his reply curt, cold. Folding his hand in a fist around a spoke, he maintained course. Settling the score would be sweet.

After he sated his lust for her over the weekend, he'd boot her out and claim his daughter.

"Hmm," she murmured, and not elaborating further, she flipped over on her stomach. Her rounded tush was an enticement, her tanned legs a jolt to his brain ... she'd wrapped them around him pulling him deeper inside her.

A roar built in his throat, and he gripped the tiller tight with his fist.

Just then, a speedboat swerved by on its way to the harbor, and the couple water skiing behind it, shouted something to him, but a squall swallowed it up. He shrugged, his mind hurling him back to the day Julia bailed on him ...

Michalis had nixed his videoconference with Tokyo and flown back to the mainland, only to find their home eerily silent. He'd taken the stairs two at a time, stomped into their bedroom and flung the closet open. Air exploded from his chest, and his heart pumped acid-spiked blood. Her clothes, her shoes, everything was still there.

He'd brushed a hand over his face, and stalked to the window with the spectacular ocean view and the Leonadis chopper parked amidst the gardens.

Could he have been wrong? Maybe she'd gone shopping—

He spun around, squinting at the top shelf of the closet. Her suitcase was missing, but not her gowns or shoes. And he knew. She was gone. A chasm gouged his insides. She couldn't even bring herself to take anything he'd given her.

Annoyed at her escapade, his intention had been to hunt her down, and demand an explanation ... haul her back home, and toss her in bed.

He rotated the helm, and a sudden gust sucked up the growl erupting from his mouth.

But when he found out she was about to cost him a marriage ... the billion Tokyo loss was incidental ... he'd been furious. But when he discovered she'd skipped out, harboring a secret— she'd hidden his own child from him, the bi— He bashed down the expletive with a snarl. Her furtive maneuver had corroded his insides and pumped him up for a major payback ...

The yacht rose on the crest of a wave and plummeted over it. He glanced at the barometer, then at her.

Poison.

She swiveled onto her back again and bending one leg, slung an arm over her eyes, her breasts rising and falling with each breath she took.

A poison he craved; he needed just a month's worth to regain his immunity.

"Mykonos Harbor to Lady One."

The radio message shattered Michalis' dark thoughts, and he seized the transmitter with such force, he nearly yanked it from its cord. "Lady One read ... copy over."

He'd named the boat Lady One for her. Foolish guy to have confessed in a moment of ardor that she'd been the one he'd waited for all his life. A muscle battered his jaw. And she'd slapped him down after only three months of matrimony.

When the story broke, every media outlet had tacked him to the wall.

"Stor ... war ..." The radio message was garbled, snapping him to attention.

"Do not copy," Michalis blasted into the mouthpiece. "Repeat."

He pumped power, increasing speed and the boat bumped

over the waves, bridging the distance to the rocky façade the sea had eroded over centuries into the shape of a mermaid.

"Hey!" Julia slid off the lounger and landed on her tush, as a strong undercurrent of air whacked her, smothering her words. "What's the big idea?" She jumped up, rubbed her bottom and marched over to him. "I—"

Her hand flew to her mouth, and the sheer beauty of the scene before her took her breath away. Against the backdrop of the coral sunset, the Mermaid's Grotto rose from the depths of the sea like a fairytale.

"You like?"

"Oh, Michalis," she said, her words hitching in her throat.

"Unusual for you to be tongue-tied." He quirked a brow, but the fleeting tilt of his mouth, tempered his words.

"It's in such high demand" —Julia smiled— "how'd you do it?"

He shrugged, inclining his head as if to say, do you need to ask?

Such arrogance ... confidence nearly left her fumbling for words. "Of course, you own the world—"

He flung back his head and laughed, the sound sending shivers shimmying up her spine.

"Only a piece of it," he quipped. "The Mermaid being part of the package."

"You bought it?"

"I did."

"Why?"

"I wanted to."

"And what you want, you get."

A long pause, and his laser-sharp eyes drilled into her. Out of bravado, Julia held his gaze and a rip of dread ... or maybe excitement licked her insides.

"Everything has a price tag."

Which meant he'd tagged her with a price. She balked at the reminder, her pulse ricocheting against her ribs. She desperately wanted to belt him with a denial, but trapped between the past and Amy's future, she had to hang tough; stay tuned to Michalis and hopefully catch a glimmer of his plans for her ... them, that might work to her benefit.

"We'll be alone here?" She averted her focus and tucked a loose curl behind her ear, her words casual. "In the middle of nowhere?

"Does that bother you?"

"Of course not," she said, but the rapid staccato of her words hinted at the possibility.

"We won't be alone, Julia," he said. "Phantom staff will service us."

"Phantom?" A nervous giggle skimmed her mouth. "You're joking."

"Nope." His hand tightened on the tiller. "The hired help will serve, but not be seen or heard."

She breathed a sigh of relief; glad she wouldn't be totally isolated on the islet with Michalis. The corner of her lip drooped. The Mermaid was only five nautical miles from Mykonos, but it might as well be in enemy waters. Fear had nothing to do with it. Temptation was totally another matter.

"A mile to go, and we'll anchor in the cove." He steered toward the coastline, and a fierce gale fueled the waves, rocking the boat off course. "What the—"

The radio crackled, "... Lady One ... warn ..."

Michalis seized the transmitter in an iron grip. "Repeat."

"Copy ... One. Freak storm ... high winds ... northwest ... due ... west."

"Copy," Michalis said, his tone grim.

"Roger ... La ... dy One."

"Something wrong?" Julia swayed closer and grabbed the door-jamb for support. The ocean smashed the yacht, white foam shooting on the deck and splashing the windshield of the control room.

Ignoring her query, Michalis staggered out to the life raft several feet away, grabbed a couple of life preservers, lurched his way back and tossed one to Julia.

"Safety precaution."

"Michalis?"

"Do it Jul—"

Another wave crashed upon the deck and washed through the doorway into the engine room, drenching them. Julia lost her balance and floundered for a handhold, but he seized her elbow, hauling her against his hip, while still controlling the wheel with his other hand.

"Get into the life jacket," he barked.

"Wha-at about you?" she stammered, slipping it over her head.

"Worried 'bout me?" A grin split his mouth, just as more waves splashed onboard.

She blinked at him, her eyes wide, lashes spiky wet, strands of hair plastered to her face. In the midst of the raging storm, he swooped down and smacked her mouth with his. "Mmm, salty."

"I can't believe you." She shook her head, droplets scattering about her and onto him.

"Believe—" The rising gale whipped through the word, but not before it lodged in her heart.

Believe.

At one time she had believed, believed with all her heart … in him … in them.

"What's left to believe, Michalis?" Her words, feather soft, were barely audible amidst the sudden ferocity of the elements, but somehow he caught them.

"Life," he growled in her ear, shackling her upper arm with his fingers.

"Ye-s," she murmured, remembering Amy.

Regardless of what happened between them, their daughter was worth fighting for, living for … believing.

Julia ripped away from his hold, staggered backward and grabbing the other life preserver, lurched forward with such force, she nearly knocked him over. He wrapped his arm around her, steadying her, and she pulled the safety jacket over his head.

"Steady." He tightened his grip across her shoulders, holding her safe in the crook of his arm. "Here comes another."

A white-capped breaker crested and crashed on deck, temporarily submerging them. She could barely breathe, but a second later she swiped saltwater from her eyes, and heaved a gallon of air into her lungs.

"Hold on, now," he shouted above nature's rage. "We'll make it."

His words offered a semblance of comfort, even amidst the onslaught of the tempest. She blinked, and the tear oozing from beneath her lashes mingled with the seawater on her face. "What happened to us, Michalis?"

"Say again?" he called, his features turning hawkish. "Don't worry, I know the sea like the back of my hand."

She nodded. "With you at the helm, I have no doubt we'll get to shore."

He snapped his head around, his eyes colliding with hers for a split millisecond, and it was like the past had never been. Before her pulse got back in sync, a giant breaker smashed the yacht and splintered them apart. Julia skidded backward, and he snaked an arm out, yanking her to his side.

"Steady there." He rounded the southwest corner of the island, and the storm pounded the yacht from all sides, driving it against the rocks.

Michalis steered away, relishing the challenge of pitting himself against the elements ... to victory. By the time Julia regained her breath, a foaming-crested monster broadsided the yacht against the submerged rocky crevice, the undercurrent pulling them under.

"Michalis!" She slammed against him, and the boat plunged and then rose, balancing on a breaker.

"Steady, Lady One," he growled, and she didn't know if he referred to the yacht or to her.

Julia didn't care, and in the sudden lull, lunged for the door. "I'm going to check—"

"Stay put." He seized her wrist with his fingers and hauled her back to his side. "Deceptive."

She snapped her head up, dazed. "Wh-hat?"

"Not me … the storm." He swiped his palm across his face, clearing his vision, and grinned.

"Let go." She pushed at him. "I want to go see—"

Another angry wave rolling toward them had her clinging to him.

"Hang on," he shouted. "We're almost out of it."

"No, Michalis!" She pointed behind her at the stairs leading down below, filling with water.

Tension tautened his cheekbones, and he propelled her in front of him.

"Take the wheel."

"I-I don't know—"

He pressed her hands on the wheel. "I'm going down to the galley to check the damage."

"Don't—" She glanced over her shoulder, but he'd already disappeared; a feeling of such devastation ripped through her that she collapsed against the wheel. But she couldn't give in to it and curling her hands over the tiller, she straightened and steered best she could.

The next few minutes seemed an eternity, and just as panic thwacked her insides, he waded upward through the flooded stairwell.

"We've got a hole starboard side," he shouted, through the rain beating down upon him. "She won't make it." His mouth set in a grim line, and then he challenged the fates, his words ringing clear above the deluge. "But we will." He blinked his waterlogged lashes, his intense gaze spearing through her. "Any doubts?"

Her lips quivered, and she shook her head, chills racking her body.

He yanked her to him and stole a kiss, his pulse pounding against hers. Just as quickly, he released her, and unhinging her numb fingers from the wheel, propelled her with him across the deck. A shudder vibrated through her, then a surprising calm spread throughout her body; she had no doubt Michalis could outmaneuver even these cataclysmic conditions.

Silly girl, to think she stood a chance of outsmarting the big man.

He tossed the anchor overboard, unhooked a coil of rope from the wall and secured one end around her waist, and the other around his. "Don't want to get separated."

A premonition or a mockery of what had become their life and what was still to be?

Lightning split the sky, and then a thunderclap accented her thoughts. A hysterical sound burst from her mouth, but the windstorm whacked it away.

"We're only half a mile from shore." Battered by the storm, he grasped her hand, dragging her with him and staggered to the edge. "The life raft would smash against the rocks and go under."

She nodded, glad she'd spent her time swimming in their private beach in Athens, while Michalis had been working overtime. She slammed her brain cells shut, not wanting to remember with whom he'd spent those late hours, when she, the ninny, had taken him at his word that he'd been working.

"Ready?" he asked, forcing her thoughts to the present.

"No-o," she said, her teeth chattering.

He tightened his grip on her fingers, and she revised her answer. "Ye-s."

At his signal, she sucked in a breath and bailed, plunging with him into the depths of the sea.

Chapter 8

Julia surfaced, gasping for air, her arms flailing, the salt water stinging her eyes.

"I've got you." Treading water beside her, Michalis swiped at his water-logged lashes to clear his vision and pointed to shore.

She nodded.

By this time, the wind had abated a bit, and Michalis strong-armed the waves with his front crawl. Julia followed, determined to keep pace with him, but she lagged several yards behind. It was like fighting a wall of water, but after what seemed like an eternity, they collapsed upon the shore, the waves washing over them.

"Okay?" he panted, his voice gravelly.

"O-okay." She coughed, flipping on her back and sucking in mouthfuls of air. "You?"

"Yeah." He nodded, and before he could reply further, the heavens opened, pelting them with wind-whipped rain.

A roll of thunder and then lightning streaked across the ink-black sky.

"Come on." He hauled her up with him and led the way up the sandy bank toward the palatial resort.

After trekking through pebbles, patches of grass and bamboo, plus the uphill battle against the rainstorm, they reached the hotel.

"Made it." He wiped rain from his face with his palm and tilted the corner of his mouth in a half grin.

"Yep." Her pulse raced, but desperately resisting his magnetic appeal, she pulled away, the rope still stretched taut between them. She yanked her life jacket over her head and worked at the knot binding her to him.

"So quick to break away." He bashed at a soaked tuft of hair flopping over his brow with his fist, and squinted at her.

A raindrop trickled down his temple, and she jerked to brush it with her fingertip, but squashed the impulse. Were his words a mere statement of fact or a query? But next moment, he assisted in the 'separation', and that put a lid on her analysis.

"Here, this is easier." He removed his life-vest, pulled out a jackknife from his back pocket and severed the twine, setting her free.

For some uncanny reason, she felt sad but she shook away the foolish feeling. She'd done 'devastatingly sad' a year ago, and finally over it, had no intention of succumbing to it again. No siree.

He slogged ahead of her, leaped up the three marble steps and pounded on the double doors with his fist. No answer. By the time she caught up to him, he'd walked the wrap-around verandah and jimmied a window open. He crawled over the windowsill, his footsteps echoing to her from inside. Seconds later, he pulled open the front doors and mocked a bow. "Welcome to my pad."

"Some pad." She elevated her shapely brow, but her mouth curved to almost a smile, and then she bit it off. No surprise, since he could afford these palatial digs three times over, just as he could a year ago. But still, curiosity got the better of her. "Bet this costs a hefty bundle in upkeep."

"A mil for this weekend at any rate." He shrugged. "But who's count—"

"A mil?" She gulped, fanning her face with her hand. "Is that all?"

He swung his head back and laughed.

That much money would be life changing to her … Amy, and most of the world, but to Michalis it was pocket change. And so the words burst out of her, "You actually dished out a million euros to get this place ready for two days just so—"

"Money well spent." He tapped the door with his palm, but his eyes narrowed a fraction. "I never make an investment without expecting a high return."

A tremor zipped through her that had nothing to do with the wet clothes clinging to her body, and everything to do with the message beneath his words. And so, she hit back, "Why splurge when we're about to—"

A deadly silence coiled them in its grip, and behind them … the lull in the elements accentuated the threat.

"About to what, Julia?" he bit out, his words steely.

"Di-divorce."

Nature unleashed its fury, the wind whooshing through the building and the rain ricocheting off the windowpanes. He grabbed her elbow to propel her inside, but the force of movement smacked her against his chest. Her nipples strained against his soaked t-shirt, and she glanced up, clashing with his dark gaze. A loaded moment, and he pivoted, shutting the doors with his shoulder against the force of wind.

Noticing the transparency of her drenched top, she stepped back and crossed her arms across her bosom. Noting her movement, he scowled and advanced back into her sphere.

"Until D-day, we'll have a last fling …" He seduced with his words, the deep timbre of his voice, his breath warming her chilled cheeks. "And make it a memorable one, mmm?"

"How could I forget the price you're demanding for a night of—?"

"Passion." He finished for her, stroking her cheek with his still damp fingers, but his heat steamed right into her, extracting the coldness from her.

"But you're wrong." His hand trailed down the curve of her jaw to her neck, every touch a flare, until he reached her cleavage, igniting a bonfire. A brush of his fingertips, a promise of what was to come. "This night ... this weekend is simply foreplay to the month ahead." He raised his hand and outlined her tremulous mouth with his thumb.

Without batting an eyelash, she made to nip his thumb, but quick on the uptake, he pulled away.

"Uh, uh." He chuckled, and she was amazed he could find anything amusing in the shipwreck of their marriage. A pause, and he bent his head, his provocative words feathering her mouth. "A taste of heaven?"

"Hell on earth, Michalis."

A gust of wind hurled against the building seeming to rock it from its foundation.

"How's it go?" Michalis leaned back and cocked a brow. "Hell hath no fury like a woman scorn—"

"I'm hungry," she blurted. "I'm going to scout around for dinner."

"—or a man taken for a fool." His barely audible warning drifted over her head, and waggling her shoulders, she meandered across the lobby, dismissing the uncanny feeling ... and him. She stepped forward, tilted her head and slanted him a curious gaze, but he'd already turned his back, marching to the front desk.

A heavy sigh struggled from deep inside her, and she rubbed the tension from her neck. Exhausted from the events of the day and the emotional tug-o-war, the plush sofa amidst the opulent décor designed with a modern slant in the spacious lobby looked most inviting. She wanted to crash out on it, close her eyes and wake up to find this nightmare gone. She wiggled a finger beneath the wet strap of her top and squirmed in her damp shorts. Too tempting, but she didn't dare stain the rich fabric with seawater.

"They bailed."

"What?" She swung around, bumped into a matching armchair and hugged it so she wouldn't sprawl over it.

"The hired help winged it to the mainland on a rescue chopper before the storm broke." He waved a note at her, and then flicked it back on the granite countertop with his thumb and forefinger. "Left dinner on the table."

"A dress up affair … dinner?" Amusement tugged the corner of her mouth, and then at the absurdity of the situation, she burst out laughing. With nothing but the clothes on their backs, they'd be hard-pressed to dress to impress.

"You have a point," he said, his eyes glinting with merriment, connected with hers.

And just for a moment, the past faded, the future too distant to contemplate, which left the present ambivalent, yet filled with possibilities.

A shutter clattered in the wind, and startled her back to her senses. She turned to resume her tour, glimpsed the telephone on the counter and vaulted for it, snatching it off the hook.

"Hello? Hello …" When no one answered, she pounded the receiver against her palm. "Come on, somebody."

"Hello, somebody," Michalis whispered in her ear, grinning.

"This is not amusing." She banged the phone down on its cradle, his warm breath tingling her skin from the roots of her hair to the tips of her toes. Because of that, and to cover her vulnerability at his nearness, she belted him with her icy glare and frosty words. "No dial tone, no way to communicate, to call and know Amy's all right."

"Amy …" —he bashed his brows over his shadowed eyes— "is safe."

"How do you know?" she asked, her voice rising.

"The nanny is m—"

"Oh, you impossible Greek." She threw up her hands and paced to and fro across the foyer. "I don't care who she is,

Michalis." She paused, a catch in her throat and a moist glint in her eye. "My child's not here with me."

"In the circumstances," he quipped, "better she's not."

A huff of a breath. "You're right, of course." It goaded her to admit it, but then she made up for it by hurling back, "How are we going to get off this piece of rock—"

He guffawed, up-staging her words, and she finished lamely, "Albeit a regal stone."

Still chuckling, he swerved behind the reception area and folded his arms on the countertop. "I'm at your service, madam."

"Michalis, how can you joke about this?" She stamped her foot on the marble tiles and her waterlogged sandal squelched; amazing she hadn't lost it in the deep. "We're stranded."

"Hardly."

"Can you get me my daughter?"

"Our daughter."

But Julia was on a roll, and distraught, she wanted to hit out … at him.

Slam him with her angst about Amy, about them … the uncertainty surrounding her, engulfing her … smothering her.

"Can you get us out of here—?" She broke off as his words pierced through the cloud of near panic. She caught her bottom lip between her teeth, and nodded. "Our child …" The words melted on her tongue, and she gaped at him standing behind the counter, his shirt plastered to his chest, the neckline rip revealing the dark sprinkle of hair she'd toyed with her fingers, her mouth … once upon a time … a forever time ago. She nearly buckled but lunged back, missed the marble pillar and clutched onto the sofa.

"Yes and yes." He bit out. "I told you, Amy is in good hands."

"Don't tell me," she let fly. "Show me."

"You think I'd endanger my own child?" His features hardened, his nose flared, and his words skimmed his tight lips. "What do you take me for?

78

She stepped up. "A double-crossing, cheat—" She swatted at him, but her hand sliced through the air.

He seized her wrist, his eyes reflecting the ferocity of the elements outside, a muscle bashing his jaw. "You're distraught—tired—"

"… no good—"

"Calm down."

"Two-timing …"

He seemed to pale around the mouth, but too worked up to give it much credence she took a second swat at him with her free hand, but he leaned away from the strike, and that infuriated her more. Within a heartbeat, he dragged her across the counter, her tongue still spitting venom.

"Thug."

"What?" The one word detonated from deep in his chest.

"Practically kidnapping me, demanding … no … exacting retribution," she hiccuped. "Plotting to take … no … buy …" Another swipe at him missed. He shackled her wrists, and she collapsed onto his chest like a rag doll, "… my daughter from me."

"You're crossing the line, *agape mou*," he bit out, his words steel, but his warning glided off her like ice melting over fire.

"I won't let you," she spat, her words muffled against his chest. "I won't, I won't." The hitch in her voice did reflect her bravado, but more her deep anxiety for her child. "She's the only family I've got."

Michalis stilled for a deafening second, and inhaling sharply, he filled his lungs, and then the air blasted from his mouth like a grenade. "I'm not … part of the family?"

"You forfeited that right when you—"

A sound sizzled between his teeth, hinting at his barely controlled emotion. It should have tipped her off, but she took no heed, all out to best him on this once.

"You used me, Julia?" he asked, his words hard, remote. "To

give you a child." Folding his fingers, he bumped his fist on his chin. "And when you got her, you slunk away like a thief in the night."

"No!" She shoved him back, but trapped between the counter and his unyielding body, she had nowhere to go. "That's a foul thing to say."

"Is it?"

"Well, what would you call it?" she flung back at him.

"This." He swooped down, his mouth devouring hers, his tongue tangling with hers, rekindling a chemical combustion of the senses.

A whimper slipped from her mouth onto his tongue, and he lapped it up. Not allowing her to come up for air, he fused her to him, her breasts pressing against his chest, his hips rocking against hers, his sex rock hard.

"Michalis, I—"

"Shh," he groaned, intensifying the onslaught on her mouth.

He nibbled his way down her chin to her throat, feasting at the pulse point, and then buried his face in her bosom. He scooped her up and stretched along with her across the counter, his hands rediscovering every inch of her body, every curve, dip and valley. Stroking her calf and exploring higher, he brushed the apex of her thighs, feathered across her navel and upward cupping her breast.

A gasp, and Julia tilted her head back, arching into him. He slipped the strap of her halter-top off her shoulder and settled his mouth on one exposed breast. He suckled, he fondled with his tongue, sending a spiral of sensation into her belly and downward where he cupped her with his other hand.

Spasms fanned inside her, and she held his head to the spot, her hands swimming through his hair, drinking him in. She'd loved this man once ... and then he ... the shadowed ache throbbed through her but was diminished by the assault on her senses.

She knew she should push him away, but her heart … her body … cried yes. Why was that?

The query flashed through her mind, then dissipated beneath his magic touch.

He flicked her nipple with his tongue, his hand across her belly sent ripples skittering through her, and she curved into him, his male strength pressing into her. Lifting his head, he captured her lips, his hips rocking against her pelvis, his signal clear.

The storm outside pummeled the palace, but it was minute compared to the tempest of the senses erupting inside between them.

"Do … you read …" the static words from the switchboard jammed through their erotic heat. "I … repeat … come in …"

"Wha-at?" Julia froze in his arms, her breath fanning his mouth.

"No," Michalis panted, tapping his forehead to hers, the denial exploding from his mouth. "No."

She wiggled beneath him, but he held her close a second longer, then heaving a mouthful of air, reluctantly released her and slid off the counter top. Cool air slapped her skin, but she barely noticed, his heat still warm upon her body.

Brushing back his still damp hair with his fingers, he blasted into the transmitter, his tone gruff, and his words gravelly. "I read you, come in."

Julia sat cross-legged on the counter and clutched her sagging top over her sensitized breasts. Licking her bottom lip, she groaned; his taste still upon her tongue. Dear God. What had she almost allowed to happen? She covered her face with her hand and her hair fell on either side, hiding the blush on her cheeks. Drawing in a forced breath, she let it slither out between her fingers; every cell in her body stimulated with sensual fervor, poised for him.

Another huff of oxygen, and she flung her head back, swung her feet over the side and wobbled to a standing position, gripping the edge of the counter to keep from crumbling to the floor.

She nearly burst out laughing at her idiotic thoughts. The danger they'd tackled out at sea must have spiked the adrenaline rush, heightening the emotion between them. Of course, it could be nothing more than that.

But then he turned, locked her with his smoldering gaze, and shattered her theory. Probing her from head to toe, he caressed her breasts with a dip of his lashes and plunged down to her half-open shorts, then shot back up to her slumberous gaze.

A flush seared her skin, and to cover the awkward moment, she blurted, "Anyone there?" Amazing and maddening that he could still make her blush, after all the sleepless nights they'd spent those first three months together, tangling beneath the sheets. The red-hot images branded her brain, and she bashed down a betraying moan.

"Nope." An unbidden smile curved his lip. "No response."

"Hit it," she said, her words emphatic. Anything to change the mood between them.

"Do what?"

"If you hit it, it jiggles the wires … that's what I do to my TV set … works every time."

"Seriously?" He chuckled, but it didn't flicker in his eyes, still dark with passion.

"Seriously." She met and held his gaze, her stomach plummeting, her pulse skyrocketing.

"To please you—" He whacked it with his palm and static sounded, but no words. "Okay, now?"

"Not okay." She bumped him aside and flicked knobs, switches then smacked the transmitter with her hand, her fist. "Hello … anybody there?" A whimper flittered from her mouth, and she slumped against the desk.

"Here, let me." Michalis took the transmitter from her nerveless fingers, his thumb stroking her palm.

"Warn … come in …"

"Yes!" Laughing, she tossed her fist in the air in victory. "Told you."

But when no other communication transmitted, her moment of elation deflated, and she braced against the counter, rubbing the chill from her arms.

"How 'bout making us a cup of coffee, while I tinker with this?"

She nodded, and trotted across the lobby to the kitchen in back, glad to keep busy. It'd keep her mind off what almost happened with her sexy ex, and placate her nerves, which were about ready to blow.

Twenty minutes later, she had a tray in hand with a pot of steaming brew and cheese and tomato sandwiches. "At least we won't starve," she muttered, but her lip quivered, fizzling her attempt to lighten the mood. A splinter of fear stabbed, but shaking it off, she marched back into the lobby.

"Dinner is served."

A crackle, a spark, and an expletive tainted the air before he flew back against the wall, groaning.

"Michalis!" She dropped the tray, and it crashed to the floor, the sound reverberating around them. Coffee aroma filled the air. She couldn't care less. Fear clawed her heart, and she rushed to him behind the reception counter, her legs wobbling.

Sprawled on the floor, he supported his forearm oozing with blood, pain carving his features.

She fell to her knees beside him. "What happened?"

Chapter 9

"I wrestled with the wires and lost." He attempted to make light of it, but his indrawn breath suggested otherwise. Clenching his teeth against the pain, he propped himself against the wall. "No big deal."

Julia took his hand and placed it over the wound. "Keep pressure on it to staunch the bleeding." Scrambling up, she raced for the bathroom and tossed over her shoulder, "I'll be right back."

Seconds later, she skidded back, plopped down beside him and opened the first aid kit with trembling hands. "Good thing I saw this when I was looking round."

"Yeah," he muttered, a stitch of pain at the corner of his mouth.

"Here let me." She took his arm, placed it across her lap and swabbed the gash clean.

He winced.

"Almost done." She picked out a roll of gauze, snipped a length with the scissors and wrapped it around his injured forearm. "You know better than to play with electrical wires," she scolded, hiding her fear behind her words.

"Someone had to fix it." He grinned. "If I didn't know better, I'd say you were concerned about me." When he saw the appalled look on her face, he shrugged, and measured a narrow space in the air with his thumb and forefinger. "Well, maybe this much, hmm?"

"Only because I didn't want to be marooned here with you."

He chuckled, and then grumbled, as she clipped the bandage together.

"Well, did you fix it?"

A bit sheepish, he shook his head. "I think the outside line may be down." He made to get up, tottered, and she reached for him, his good arm encircling her shoulders, his warmth seeping into her. "Without a flashlight, it'll have to wait 'til morning." His fingers feathered across her nape, sending tingles of awareness through her. "You don't happen to have one in your back pocket do you?"

She shook her head, fighting off a quiver at the corner of her mouth. "You okay now?"

"Good to go." He stood firmly on his feet, but still held onto her. "Without electricity, we'll have to be creative in amusing ourselves for the night."

She disengaged from his embrace and took a pace back, hands on hips. "Exactly what does that mean?" As if she didn't know. Their bantering was simply a delay of the inevitable. A tremor ripped through her. Michalis would collect his due.

Her.

He turned an innocent face her way. "Why, we'll dine on sandwiches and coffee" —a quick glance at the food strewn on the floor— "to the serenade of the wind 'n surf whooping it up outside."

A whoosh of sound slammed against the windows, followed by a crash; and the remaining lights flickered and went out.

Julia screamed, her hands fluttering to her mouth.

"Hey, it's just the shutters." He encircled her shoulders with his good arm and drawing her closer, stroked her hair with his fingers.

For a second, she accepted the reprieve of his touch … okay

two, three seconds, and then she drew in a shaky breath and exhaled.

"I'm cool now." She patted his biceps and stepped away, her fingertips tingling from the contact on the iron hard muscle.

"Really?"

"Ye-eah."

"Can't see two inches in front of my face," he rasped, "but I can still feel. And baby doll, your ... er ... cool's singeing right through my shirt."

"I ... uh ... saw some candles in the kitchen drawer earlier," she said, avoiding his bait. "I'll go—"

"No, stay put," he commanded. "I'll go."

While he bumped his way through the lobby to the kitchen, Julia felt her way across the foyer and collapsed on the sofa. About to leap up, she shrugged, exhausted; maintenance could deal with any possible sea stains.

The minutes ticked by, and she rubbed her arms to chase the chill away, although it was more a reaction from what had just transpired than feeling cold. The balmy night was a blessing. Electricity might be on the blink, but at least they weren't going to freeze.

"Got it." The sound of his voice sent a spark of relief through her, underscoring the sliver of excitement prodding her, but she vehemently denied the latter.

He strolled back with two lit candles on a tray of fresh sandwiches and two mugs of steaming coffee.

"You'll hurt your arm carrying—" She sprang up to help, but he waved her back down.

"Arm's ... uh ... cool."

"Good to know." She shifted on the sofa and ignored his verbal baiting.

He set the tray on the accent table and sank down beside her, the cushions dipping beneath his weight. "Have a sandwich."

"Thanks." She picked one up and bit into it, relishing the taste. "Mmm, this is good."

"Sure is," he chomped into his sandwich, and winked.

By the glint in his eye, she knew time was running out. The food turned tasteless in her mouth, and she swallowed, a morsel snagging in her throat. She reached for the coffee cup.

He seized his cup and clinked it with hers. "Cheers, Julia—"

"Here's to a quick rescue." She raised her cup, took a gulp and wheezed.

"Hey, are you alright?" He took the cup from her hand, set it on the tray and patted her back.

"I-I'm fi-ine." She coughed, her eyes watering, and waved him away.

Tentatively she took another sip of the bittersweet brew, and although it stung her raw throat, she forced it down.

He drained his cup, studied her over the rim, and then set it on the table. "It won't be long."

"For what?" She replaced her half-eaten sandwich and half-full cup of coffee on the tray and folded her hands in her lap.

He inclined his head, toward the door. "The rescue you've been pining for."

A sigh of relief preempted the nervous giggle scratching her throat. "Oh, that."

"Yes, that." He stroked his chin with the back of his hand. "But we still have the night, maybe two before—"

She shot up, debating her course of action. He was toying with her, like the cat that had the canary cornered, then pounced. Foolish thought. Michalis didn't pounce, he seized, he—

"The lady has to be willing, Julia."

"Yes, she does, Michalis," she whispered. "A-and, I don't think this is a good idea."

He hauled himself from the sofa and in two steps bridged the gap between them, standing so close his heat radiated to her, his fresh ocean scent wrapping around her like a long forgotten memory. A shift of his stance, and his shorts brushed the hem of her own, but still he did not touch her. Awareness flared between them, his potent sexuality a catalyst to her own.

"On the contrary," he murmured, his breath caressing her cheek. "It's an excellent idea."

Silence enveloped them, severed only by the storm outside.

Julia could not move. The candlelight flickered, casting shadows across his proud features; she'd touched, kissed every spot, plane, line, angle of his face; the tiny scar at the cleft of his chin. She wrinkled her brow. He'd never told her how he'd gotten it. So much she didn't know about him. And now she'd never know. A pang of regret pierced her. A million years had passed since then, and she banished the bittersweet memory with her impersonal words.

"I-I'll clear this up." She reached across him for the tray, but he stayed her hand, curling his fingers around hers, his thumb stroking her palm.

"Julia—"

"Michalis—"

She jolted upward and bumped his forehead. Her giggle mingled with his chuckle and shattered the awkward moment.

"It's been a long day." She brushed her hand across her brow, and a tired sigh slipped from her mouth. "I'm going up to bed."

"A good idea." He shot her a killer smile and in the eerie light, it looked more like a leer. "I'll come up and join you as soon as I've checked the premises."

"You have a choice of rooms."

"I do," he said, tone wolfish. "Yours."

Sunlight warmed her eyelids, and Julia stretched her limbs beneath the covers. Although her muscles were still a bit tense, a smile curved her mouth. Michalis must've made another choice, since the bed had been hers alone all night. A giggle reared, but she muffled it with her hand. He hadn't had much choice against a locked door, had he?

You think a bolted door would keep a man like Michalis out? The silent query zapped her mind, and she shrugged. So, she'd get a night's reprieve. She bounced on the mattress. "Mmm, like sleeping on a cloud."

She fluttered her eyelashes open, and peered through the crack in the lace curtains of the French doors leading to the wrap-around terrace. Blue sky, sunshine and the sound of surf lapping the shore made for a sparkle of a day. The antithesis of the night before. A yawn, and she hopped out of bed, padded across the room and curling her toes on the plush carpet, pulled the curtains aside.

"Oh my," she gasped, a jab in her stomach, a jig in her heart and a blush coating her body. "A Greek god surfacing from the depths of the sea."

Totally nude, Michalis waded from the foam of the sea, dragging something with him and tossing it on the sand. Then he dove back, surfaced and tossing his head back, swam to the cabin cruiser, miraculously still buoying above the water. After watching him for a few minutes, she turned away and dressed in her shorts and top. A quick freshen up in the luxurious bathroom, and barefoot, she ventured down the winding staircase, untangling her hair with her fingers.

She opened the front doors and stepped onto the balcony. Sunlight glinted on the ocean; the breeze was fresh upon her face, a seagull sailed across the sky. She lifted her hands to heaven, thankful, and breathed the clean sea air.

When she dropped her arms to her sides, she scanned the sea for Michalis but he was nowhere in sight. A prick of fear had her jumping the three steps, her feet sinking in the sand, the warmth a surprise so early in the morning. But oh, so soothing.

Lifting a hand, she shaded her eyes against the glare of sunlight and caught sight of him further along the shore dragging another item from the waves. A sense of peace permeated through her, and leaving him to salvage the bounty from the yacht, she trudged through the sand to a spot half hidden by overhanging rock and brush interspersed with bamboo.

For a moment she stood, listening to the force of nature crashing upon the rocks, then the seagull squawked and landed several yards away, scavenging for breakfast.

She ignored the rumbling in her stomach, and blotted her upper lip already beading with perspiration. Jiggling her blouse sticking to her skin, she hesitated a second, and then flinging off her clothes, plunged into the sea. The water glided off her shoulders like silk. She swam out a little way and flipped on her back, squinting at the seagull now flying through the seeming endless blue sky. Sea and sky merged, and she closed her eyes, floating on the gentle waves.

"Mmm, heaven."

"So, it is,"

He pulled her under, her hair floating around her, and scrambling, she shot upward, splashing water everywhere.

"Michalis, how—" she spluttered, wiping the sea-sting from her eyes.

"I couldn't let a mermaid frolic in the ocean alone." He trod water beside her, a twinkle in his eye and a chuckle on his lips.

Seawater dripped from his hair to his cheeks, streaming down his pectorals and plastering the sprinkle of hair cushioning the crucifix he wore. He'd told her that at seventeen, he'd been beachcombing and found it washed upon the shore. A good omen, he'd whispered in her ear so long ago.

"Especially if she's my mermaid."

"I'm not yours." Twisting away, she bashed the sentimental thoughts far back into her mind. At that age while he roamed the beach carefree, she'd been stuck in foster care waiting for her mom to come for her. Although she'd promised, Lolita had never shown up; at least not for her daughter.

Julia had soon learned not to hold her breath, waiting for her mother. She couldn't depend on her mother, and had learned to fend for herself. Luckily, a talent scout had come to her high school one day ... and thereafter, she soon discovered the brutal world of high fashion where she could only depend upon herself. And except for a rare friend like Chachee, no one else.

A glance at Michalis from beneath her damp lashes triggered a stitch of pain inside her. She'd dropped her façade for him, relying on him, trusting him, loving him—

"You are my mermaid for the month."

His words were like a splash of ice water, splattering her thoughts. Apparently history wasn't done yet, for here she was with Michalis who still called the shots. And to get back at him, she splashed him, and swam for shore. He gave chase with his strong front crawl and quickly overtaking her, scooped her up in his arms and marched through the foam of surf to the beach.

"Let me go."

"Sure thing." A heavy breath, and he trudged through the sand, skirting a sandy knoll and plunked her on a towel, half shaded by a screen of bamboo. Dropping down beside her, he twirled a wet strand around his index finger, and then dipped his head, nuzzling her neck, nipping her earlobe. A flicking of his tongue behind her ear triggered a spiral of sensation inside her.

"Michalis, please—"

"Michalis, please what?" he murmured, the words a guttural sound from deep in his chest.

She raised her hands to push him away, but he caught them with his, wrapping them around his neck. "Mmm, you smell good." He bumped his nose to hers, his mouth smiling against hers, his warm breath a caress upon her face. "Fresh, clean and natural." He flicked the tip of his tongue on her lips, and smacked his own. "Got to do something about that salt, though."

And suddenly she laughed—and didn't know why ... didn't care—the sound ringing loud and clear in the lazy day. "Well, that lets me off the hook." She wiggled beneath him, but he held her steady beneath his body.

"Oh ho no," he chuckled. "I can get used to extra seasoning."

He nibbled his way down her throat, to the swell of her breast, covering one with his hand while dallying with the other with his tongue.

A tightening in her belly gave rise to sexual desire, stimulating her every cell. She arched into him, sucking in a breath, her fingers stroking the damp hair at his nape, the muscles of his back, trailing over his shoulders to his biceps. A purr of sound from deep in her throat, and for a moment, she wanted to succumb to the erotic feel of his skin upon hers, his leg stretched between hers, his hair a welcome abrasion on her thighs, igniting what was on the brink of exploding between them.

"But I can't."

"Really?" he murmured into her neck. "You seem to have been doing just fine a moment ago."

"I'm … er … hungry." She glanced up at him, stroking her fingers along his angular jaw to the cleft of his chin. "What's for breakfast?"

He hiked a brow, a saucy grin on his mouth, and she knew she'd walked into that one.

Amusement twitched her mouth, and she placed her hand on his chest, attempting to resist him. "Real food, Michalis." The words were a whiz of breath between her lips.

"Exactly what I had in mind, soul food." He propped himself on his elbow, watching her, his forefinger traveling down her cleavage, across her belly, flirting with her navel. A heavy beat, and he spanned his hand across the curls at the apex of her thighs. "Julia," he rasped, his gaze clouding with passion.

She tangled her fingers in the damp curls on his chest, his heart pounding beneath her hand. "Oh, Michalis—"

He hauled her into his arms, his mouth devouring hers … his tongue plunging into her mouth, his hips pressing into hers.

Dear God, she was on fire with him, and felt for sure any minute they'd incinerate in a detonation of the senses. He rocked with her to the rhythm of the waves crashing upon the rocks, and on the brink of no return, he gripped her shoulders, and an epithet blasted from his mouth.

"Bad timing."

A whirring noise penetrated through the haze of passion, then a shout from the approaching chopper. "Ahoy down there."

Julia stilled in his arms, and he shifted, shielding her with his body. "That guy's fired." A heave of a breath, and he reluctantly pulled away, and then paused at the panic look on her face.

"What?"

"My clothes."

He nodded, tossed her his shirt hanging from a bamboo shoot and slipped into his shorts. Planting a quick kiss on her mouth, he took her hand and jogged with her to a clearing on the beach, waving.

"We see you," the pilot announced hovering overhead.

In a daze, Julia wondered how being with Michalis could feel so right in her heart and so wrong in her mind. Before she could formulate an answer, the chopper began its descent, and he pulled her into the crook of his arm, protecting her from the flying sand.

Her pulse kicked into high gear, the traitorous image branded on her brain, hurling to the forefront of her memory and lacerating her emotions anew. A tear trickled from the corner of her eye. She'd seen him with her. Surely, her eyes couldn't lie, could they?

Chapter 10

"Amy!" Julia leaped from the limo as soon as it swerved into the driveway, and snatched her daughter from the nanny's arms. Barely glancing at the nanny, she showered the child with kisses, and gave the sitter a quivery smile. "Thank you." A pause, a frown, and the question shot from her mouth. "But how did you know we'd be here so soon?"

"Michalis." The young woman glanced his way from beneath her huge sunhat, her body language speaking volumes, and then she hurled herself into his arms.

A flash of memory, but Julia shook her head, unable to grasp it.

"Hey, nothing to worry about." He held onto her a little too long, his eyes clashing with Julia's over the girl's head.

Julia's stomach dove, and there went that clenching in her belly again.

Dismissing the uneasy feeling, she held onto her baby, glad to be in Athens, and closer to the airport.

"You gave us all a scare," the girl said, her words muffled against his sleeve. "Are you alright?"

"Better, actually." He winked.

Julia shot him an astounded look, and he grinned.

"Fresh sea air, a beautiful woman by my side—"

"Okay, you needed some time off." Smiling, she tossed Julia a surreptitious glance. "He works much too hard, don't you think?" She hooked her arm through his and strolled right by her and Amy toward the house. "Where's Mario?"

"Had to get back to the office."

Julia followed them inside and paused in the foyer, a nerve ticking at her temple. "I think I'll get Amy ready for her nap." She stepped onto the stairwell and turned to climb the stairs.

"Lunch will be served on the patio," the young woman announced, seeming more like the owner than the sitter. "I figured you'd be hungry after all that excitement."

"Thank you, but I'm not very hungry," Julia murmured over her shoulder.

"Come, Julia," Michalis said, patting the other woman's hand. "Can't disappoint …" He inclined his head at Maria, draped on his arm. "You haven't eaten all morning."

"I've left Amy's things in the nursery," the nanny said, then clapped her hands. "We'll have a party." She nodded, her brown curls bobbing beneath her hat and her eyes alight with energy. A celebration for your safe return and a warm-up for our wed—"

"If you'll excuse me." Julia fled up the stairs and dashed into the nursery, holding Amy close to her heart. Seismic shocks vibrated through her, and she sagged against the closed door, the shadowed images in her mind clearing; she'd seen them together, her running from the bedroom into Michalis' arms. A whimper sounded from her mouth. She'd died that day.

Amy gurgled and squirmed in her arms, and she loosened her grip just a bit.

How could Michalis hire his mistress as the nanny for their child? And if that hadn't been enough, how could he be planning to marry the girl while dallying with her, Julia? What kind of a man had he become? Had he always been a louse? And she, the naïve fool hadn't caught on until it had been too late.

Her stomach roiled, and she sucked in oxygen, chasing blackness from her eyelids. And what did that make her? She'd agreed to this proposition, hadn't she?

For Amy. The whisper-soft words eased her conscience.

She caressed the baby's head, and choking down the bitter taste sheathing her tongue, found solace in hugging her child. If she hadn't had to keep upright to protect Amy, she would have slithered to the floor, raw pain washing over her and leaving her numb. But she didn't have that luxury, so on seemingly wooden legs she walked to the crib to attend to her child.

Minutes later, the door clicked open, and she looked up from changing Amy, her heart faltering. "I can manage, thanks."

"No doubt." Michalis stood gripping the doorframe unable to take his eyes off his wife and child. Regret slammed his gut. He took a step closer, wanting to enfold them both in his embrace, and somehow ease the widening rift between him and Julia.

"Why'd you rush off like that?" he demanded, scowling. So much for good intentions.

"You need to ask?"

"I do."

Instead of answering his question, she batted him a level look and provoked him with a question of her own. "What do you want?"

He wanted a lot of things, but one look at her set face and he realized this wasn't the time to tell her. "I've accepted the dinner invite for us."

"I'm sure you'll both have a nice time."

"Of course—" He lowered his lashes, his narrow focus tacking her to the crib post. "Okay, spill."

"It's the nanny, Michalis, isn't it?"

"Of course, it's the nanny." A perplexed look crossed his features. "You already know that."

She paled, and her lip trembled. "You admit it … finally?"

"Yes." A line carved his forehead. "You heard her, she's giving a party for—"

"I heard."

"You'll come?"

"No."

"You'll disappoint our nanny."

A brittle laugh. "You mean *your* nanny."

"Enough, Julia." He took a deep breath, exhaled a typhoon and paused, debating. Then, "She's not *my* nanny as you term it. She's my—"

"You'd better go," she said, her words frosty. "You don't want to disappoint her."

"She's expecting us."

"You'll have to go alone." She reached for the baby's bottle and, squirting a drop on her inner wrist, tested the temperature. "I'm busy."

"I'll take Amy and—"

"No!"

"—you can meet us next door later."

She held up her hand, swallowed and swatted a loose curl off her brow. "I'd rather not."

"I'll wait 'til you're ready." He plunked down on the plush armchair in the corner and crossed one leg over the other, like he had all the time in world. See what she made of that. "We'll go together."

"No we won't," she said, voice firm. "The noise, the music … she needs to sleep."

The child sat in the middle of the crib, gurgling and playing with a soft toy.

"Seems like Amy's ready to party."

Julia gawked at him. "You're unbelievable."

"Then, you'll join me … us?" he asked, the words snapping off his tongue, his gaze slitted. "Won't you?"

She shook her head and settling Amy beneath the blanket,

stroked her cheek with her forefinger. "I can't leave her again."

"All right, Julia," he said, a sigh bursting from his mouth. "*Kyria Phytakis*, the housekeeper will watch her here."

"You go." She adjusted the cover across the baby's shoulders and turning a stiff back to him, gave Amy her bottle. "I'll watch my child."

"Amy's not a possession, Julia."

"Does that go for you, too, Michalis?" She spun around, her eyes flashing fury, her breasts rising and falling.

He was mesmerized. So beautiful and yet behaving like a shrew. Or was that only where he was concerned? The possibility didn't sit well with him, and he swung back. "I want what's best for her."

"Then let us alone."

He laughed, a dry sound. "Not just yet."

She pursed her lips, her eyes narrowed. "Does that mean you will … let us go?"

He quirked a brow.

A high-strung sound stung her mouth. "Of course, you won't."

"You're free to go, Julia," he said, his jaw tense, his eyes granite hard. "Amy stays with me."

You proud Greek, that's not how to win her confidence. Savagely, he shut his mind to the jab.

"You'll be late for the party," she said, sweetly.

"It won't be the same without you," he retorted in kind, then almost retrieved his words. What was this, high school? He shook his head, amazed how grown-ups could make such a mess of things. Correction; how he and Julia had made a mess of things. Okay, grown-ups.

"Really, Michalis," she whispered. "You take my breath away."

"It's a dress up affair," he said, rubbing the back of his neck. "A couple of hours next door."

"You'll be next door," she reiterated. "I'll be right here with my daughter."

"And mine."

She shrugged.

"Woman, you're trying my patience."

A sliver of laughter sounded from her, and it only spurred his frustration.

"Julia, you forget we have a deal."

"Flexing muscle, Michalis?"

"I prefer to call it common sense." He scrubbed his face with his palm. "And a gentle reminder."

"Huh!" she exclaimed. "More like a weight over my head."

"Come now, Julia," he said, hauling himself from the chair. "You're being overdramatic."

"The drama's just got started ... er ... continues."

"I can hardly wait," he mocked, striding to the door.

"Well, you'll have to."

"Eight this evening." And with that departing shot, he exited, clicked the door shut behind him and whistled his way down the stairs.

At seven-thirty that evening, Julia sat on the bed still not dressed for the party; her clothes strewn everywhere. She couldn't stomach watching him and the nanny ... the next Mrs. Leonadis and stepmom to Amy, canoodling. A giggle teased her lips, but it morphed into a quiver, and her shoulders sagged.

Had she actually thought the word 'canoodling?' That's a Chachee word. She sighed, missing her friend and her life in Paris; as threadbare as it had been, it had been hers ... she'd been in control. Now, she felt caught in a storm without a rudder, drifting aimlessly.

She shifted through the dresses, and tossed one after the other aside. To regain her emotional equilibrium and control of her life, she had to get far and away from Michalis Leonadis. A coward's way out? She shrugged, preferring to think of it as avoiding temptation. Temptation that she might allow something to happen between them that she'd later regret.

Somehow, she had to make her getaway without him being the wiser. If he caught her … her heart palpitated, panic pricking her insides and for a second immobilizing her … he'd take Amy away from her.

Pensively, she rose from the bed and picking up another gown, turned, catching her reflection in the mirror; she looked as disheveled as she felt. Well, she wouldn't pull it off looking like something the cat dragged in.

She shouldn't care. Not give a hoot about Michalis and his *nanny*. But the rub was, she did.

And so how to play this evening? This could very well be the last time she 'dressed up' for him, and she wanted to pull out all the stops. Knock him for six. She wanted to feel empowered, look smashing and leave him regretting that he'd tossed her aside. Yeah, she could then walk away vindicated.

He'll have you for the month still, the voice in her head needled. She shut out the taunt, and scooping up a sapphire-colored gown, twitched her nose and hurled it aside. "No, he won't." The words whisper-soft from her lips were scored with a hard edge. She'd find an escape route before then, and in a way that didn't jeopardize Amy's future.

She had to.

Swaying before the mirror, she inclined her head, contemplating. Should she dress as the mannequin … every man's fantasy? Or the woman she was … one man's desire? She picked up another dress and held it up before the full-length mirror, jumping at the knock on the door.

"*Kyrios* Leonadis is expecting you in ten minutes, *Kyria* Leonadis," the maid called from behind the panel.

Hearing the maid address her as Mrs. Leonadis gave her a jolt, and she blinked the sting of tears from her eyes. If she let her imagination run away, she could almost believe … No! That would lead to disaster for sure. Squashing the silk in her hands, she straightened her shoulders and bashed the foolishness from her mind. "I-I'll be down shortly."

In the end, she decided on the scarlet. He'd brought her here to play the scarlet woman for the month, so she might as well have the glam rags to match. The body-hugging sheath with peek-a-boo slits allowed a glimpse of leg to her thigh, a slash across her cleavage tantalized and another sliced down her back to her posterior for added shock effect.

She swept her hair up to one side and secured it with a diamond clip, wisps of curls caressing her cheek. Leaving her throat bare, she clipped elongated sparkles on her earlobes and strapped a matching bracelet on her wrist.

A twinge of regret, and she flexed her bare fingers. She'd hurled her wedding ring across their bedroom that last day, but for some reason now felt naked without it. A nervous giggle skimmed her mouth. Well, hardly that, although a bit risqué would be right on; she brushed a hand over her hip and twisted, studying her reflection in the mirror. She shrugged, slipped her feet into stilettos, and picked up her evening bag.

A heave of a breath, and then another. "Come on, you can do this." A second later, she glided out of the room and down the stairs. When she reached the bottom step, she gripped the banister, not wanting to let go.

"Julia." Michalis stood in the center of the floor, her name a soft caress from his lips. His eyes glittered, and he lowered his lashes, eclipsing the desire in them.

An air pocket expanded inside her but dissolved in her throat before it burst from her in frustration. Definitely her imagination was working overtime, but his magnetism drew her in, even as she resisted the pull. Dressed in designer slacks, matching jacket and a silk shirt unbuttoned halfway to his waist, he stole her breath.

"Michalis." She tightened her grip on the banister, his name a breath of sound from her mouth. How was she going to get through the evening with her sexy husband, who wasn't really hers? Had he ever been? Her nerves bopped, her stomach flipped and her mind reeled.

Twenty-seven days left.

Could she carry out the ruse for that long, if he stonewalled her attempt to escape tonight?

"Yoo hoo, Michalis, Julia," Maria waved, dressed in classic black with flecks of gold. "Over here."

Michalis grasped Julia's elbow, guiding her through the gathering party goers, an austere look on his features. A waiter placed a champagne flute in her hand, and she accepted it—hey, she was here to play a part, so she might as well go with it. Michalis, on the other hand, declined a drink.

When they reached the girl, Maria closed her eyes and swayed to the *bouzouki* music, humming beneath her breath. "Remember this?" She lifted her lashes, a mischievous look in her pupils, and grabbed his arm. "Come."

Michalis shot a look at Mario leaning negligently against a marble mantle by the blazing fire. His legal whiz raised his glass and grinned.

Time to canoodle.

Maria snuggled up to Michalis, and pushed him onto the dance floor as the tempo of the music picked up to a traditional Greek folk dance. Clapping, the crowd formed a circle around them and shouted, "*Opa!*"

Finally, the melody reached a crescendo and the dance ended. A radiant Maria threw herself into his arms and kissed his cheek. "I can still out maneuver you on the dance floor," she teased.

"Thanks I get for teaching you the moves." Michalis tapped the tip of her nose with his thumb, placed his hands on her shoulders and turned her toward Mario.

Michalis' words conjured up illicit scenes ... Julia backed further away, blood draining from her face, chills invading her body. Her barely touched champagne swished in the glass, and she set it on a nearby table, thankful for the wall propping her back. After all this time, she'd come face to face with the other woman once again; amazing she hadn't recognized her at the start.

A cynical sound slid between her teeth. Of course, the hat, the sunglasses should've tipped her off, but she hadn't expected Michalis to stoop so low. Hiring his mistress as the nanny for their child and keeping her living practically under their roof. She was about to be sick. Bile rose in her throat and perspiration broke out on her upper lip. An anguished cry burst from her, and pressing a hand to her mouth, she glanced around for an escape.

"Julia?" Mario stepped up beside her and brushed her shoulder. "Is something wrong?"

Michalis glanced her way, pinning her to the spot, the smile swiped from his mouth. A frown creased his forehead. Gently, he nudged Maria toward Mario, and took a step to bridge the gap between them.

Frantic, Julia pushed away from the wall, and meandered through the milieu of people until she found solace on the terrace. It didn't last. Hushed voices floated to her, barely audible amidst music and chatter sailing out from the main salon.

"A nice couple ... marriage ... good ..."

From beneath her lashes, Julia peered at the women sitting at a table in the corner, and the words on the tip of her tongue, 'wouldn't recommended it,' morphed into a brittle laugh. Everything was a blur of emotion and pain. She clutched the rail, staring far out to sea, then glanced up at the star-studded sky.

"The groom ... disentangle ... to get her." A laugh. "A nice story."

Who were these busybodies gossiping about? Bits of their hushed chatter drifted to her, and having heard enough, Julia closed her eyes and swayed to the music floating onto the terrace. Scent of jasmine permeated the air around her, and she was thankful the plant's leafy stems coiled around the trellis, concealing her from their sight.

"… Leonadis on full throttle."

The gossipers' words nearly felled her, and she sagged against the twisted iron rods, drawing deep breaths of the night air. Prickles of awareness rose all over her body, and she sensed him before she saw him.

"Something wrong?" Michalis reached her side, a puzzled look on his face.

"No," she croaked, then cleared her throat. "Of course not." She flashed him a strained smile, her nerves twittering, her palms damp and her thoughts swirling. "Michalis *mou*." She forced the endearment from her numb lips and touched his forearm. "Everyone seems to be having a nice time."

"Except you?"

She gaped at him, words frozen on her tongue.

"Julia …"

"If you'll excuse me, I need to freshen up."

He lowered his lashes a tad, trapping her in his narrow focus. "Will you get me a drink?"

"Of course." But for a long moment, he didn't move, studying her beneath his brows. When she took a step to go, he inclined his head and placing his hand at the small of her back, escorted her inside.

Skin on skin.

She gritted her teeth against the high voltage shooting up her spine from his touch, and paused center floor of the salon. Tossing him a tremulous smile, she made a beeline for the bathroom, her peripheral vision keeping him within sight. On his way to the bar, friends and colleagues intercepted him to have a word, but smoothly he disengaged himself from his fans.

104

Mario and Maria approached him, gesturing her way. She waved, smiled and got lost in the crowd.

Julia kept walking, past the powder room, the coat check and straight out the door, down the back stairs and into the starlit night.

Loosening his tie, Michalis stomped across the foyer of his home and paused at the foot of the stairs. Just hours ago, he'd stood there, mesmerized by Julia in that risqué rag descending the stairs. At that time, his heart pounded and his gut had hitched as it did now. But for different reasons.

He'd been a fool thinking she'd worn it for him … other than to provoke him. A hint of a smile. At least he'd gotten a reaction from her, a degree warmer than the cold shoulder she'd been giving him from the moment they'd stepped onto the dry land of the Leonadis estate.

The smile vanished from his mouth, and he inflated his lungs, his pulse thrashing in his throat. He'd been ready to take her right there on the floor. A wry chuckle skimmed his tight lips. Hadn't he learned anything in this last year?

If Julia was dolled up in threads more suited for the catwalk than a party, she'd had an agenda. An agenda, that more than likely didn't include him.

And yours included her, right? He bashed the irritant from his mind, and stamped on the first step of the staircase.

He swiped away the sweat beading on his forehead with the back of his hand. It was time to lay his cards on the table with his wife … er … the fashion queen, and see if something could be salvaged between them, one way or another. For Amy's sake.

The thought of his child melted his heart, and about to climb the stairs, he paused. A nightlight at the foot of the stairs cast shadows about him. It was quiet. He frowned. Too quiet. His mind replayed another time … his abs tightened, and he flexed his hands.

He swore and leaped up the stairs, kicking the bedroom door open.

"Julia!"

Deafening silence.

She was gone.

The realization crashed over him before he turned on the light. She'd given him the slip once again, and worse. His heart pounded in his ears, and he rushed into the nursery. A blue streak fueled the air.

His daughter was gone.

He glanced at the Cartier watch strapped to his wrist. Twenty minutes ago. If he hadn't spent time chatting with Mario and Maria at the bar, they would've collided at the door.

"Some scene that would've been," he muttered, curling his lip in contempt. Flipping on his cell phone, he instructed his security to keep her under surveillance, not to make an approach, but to report her every move.

He pounded his fist on the wall. The woman would be the end of him if he didn't wrap this up soon. And her timing was the pits.

If he chased after her now, there would be another deal in the tank. This one was extra padding for Amy's trust fund … and so the fashion diva could stew for a while longer. If she knew him at all, she'd know they'd have a confrontation soon enough. In the meantime, he'd seal the business deal, ensure Mario had the paperwork in order, and then he'd take great pleasure in dealing with his ex.

Pocketing his phone, he stomped across the room and stepped onto the balcony, scent of orange blossom wafting over him. He barely noticed; every muscle in his body was coiled for action.

By month's end, Julia Armstrong Leonadis would be officially his ex, since she wanted it that way. Acid curdled his gut. He wanted it that way too, didn't he?

A blast of a breath, then his heart booted his ribs in protest, giving him the answer. Brooding, he looked across the ocean, barely visible in the darkness, except for the glimmer of lights in the distance from the ships, including two from the Leonadis Cruise Line, docked at Piraeus harbor.

An image of his uncle and his Lolita taunted his mind. He spun around in distaste and stalked back inside, his foot bumping the blanket on the floor. He stooped to pick it up, and the scent of baby powder nearly made him double over. Squinting, he swept up the crinkled photo from beneath, and got torpedoed.

"What the—?" The American Lolita stared up at him, and her words, '*With Love to my Julia,*' barbed in his flesh. "*Theos mou,*" he muttered.

There was an explosion inside him, and he dropped the photo, watching it flutter to the floor. He felt a strong temptation to stamp on it with his shoe, but didn't move. How in hell had he missed the signs? How in hell could he *not* have missed the signs? He'd had no clue, none. And to a man of his stature, that didn't go down well. He shoved his hands in his pockets and prowled the floor; the tendons in his neck tightening, his fury folding his face with each step he took.

"Triple threat indeed," he growled. But she'd be on the receiving end this time. For some reason, even that notion left no satisfaction. He tautened his abs, and a sliver of common sense pierced his black mood. She'd wanted nothing from him, other than the child. She'd been willing to 'sell herself' to him for her child. Could he be wrong about her?

"Oh, yeah," he ground out, crushing the jolt to his conscience. She'd left, taking nothing from him except what he valued most. His daughter.

His eyes slitted, his jaw turned iron hard. "He'd know the truth soon enough."

Just then his cell rang, tearing his thoughts apart. "Leonadis," he barked. "Good work." Exactly as he figured, she'd ditched Athens for Paris.

He backtracked from the room, changed his mind, strode back

and snatching up the picture, stuffed it in his pocket. "A reminder," he sneered.

He stalked out and down the hall, taking the stairs two at a time. He had to take care of his daughter ... keep her far away from Julia, the Parisian Lolita. A cruel laugh detonated from his chest, ripping through the silence of the house. He had no qualms about keeping company with his Parisian Lolita, for as long as it suited him.

Chapter 11

Ring, ring!

Groggy from the emotional stress of the last few days, Julia pushed her head under the pillow of her daybed in her matchbox pad behind the Rue Royale, muting her moan.

"Go away," she mumbled, pain nipping her cells. "I don't want to talk to anybody. Not see anyone."

How could she have made such a mess of her life?

Ring, ring! She snatched the cell phone from the bedside table and blasted, "I'm not home." Then, she flipped on her back and chuckled at the affronted voice from the other line telling her to get her butt in gear; she was needed.

"G'morning, Chachee." She yawned and pushing her hair off her face, shuffled up on one elbow. "How'd you know I was back?"

"Doesn't matter." He brushed her query aside, his voice filtering through the airwaves. "How soon can you get over to the salon?"

"Would next week do?" She pulled the blanket to her chin, huddling beneath. "I only just got here three days ago, and was hoping to—" What she had to do was regroup, decide her course of action, and seek legal counsel. Which would be expensive.

More money she didn't have. She sighed. For sure, Michalis would do battle with her. It was simply a question of when.

And she had to be ready for him.

"*Non*, today, *s'il vous plaît*."

"Aww, Chach, I can't."

'I'm calling in a favor, *chéri*," he said, his words crackling over the line.

"Oh, Chachee," she murmured, pouting. "Have you no heart?"

"I guess not." He laughed, and that had her chuckling. "See you in an hour."

"Once I've called Mrs. Knightley to babysit, I'll be over for a run through." She keyed off the connection, glanced at Amy sleeping soundly in her cot, and sniffed, blinking tears pressing against her eyelids. God help her, she had to find a way to make this work out for her child, and still leave herself heart-whole; and not at the mercy of Michalis Leonadis.

At eleven that morning, Julia hopped from the Metro and trekked the remaining few blocks in her sturdy boots, passing the flower carts parked on street corners, the *boulangerie-pâtisseries* with window displays of fresh-baked *baguettes* and pastries. Across the street, the outdoor cafés were filled with chattering patrons, and the scent of freshly brewed coffee filled the air.

"Mmm, yum," she murmured, but unable to stop and indulge, wove her way around the pedestrians.

She swung her hefty-sized bag over her shoulder; glad she'd thrown on her blazer over her jeans and pullover. A misty sun struggled through the clouds, but the nip in the air won out. But in Greece the sun shone—the combustible attraction between her and Michalis on the beach at the Mermaid's Grotto had almost incinerated her, and she would've succumbed if the rescue chopper hadn't interrupted them. A whimper sounded from her mouth, and shivering, she shoved her hands in her pockets, shutting her mind to the seductive memories.

A second later, she turned the corner of Avenue Montaigne, the glitzy venue of luxury brands such as Dior, Chanel; side-stepping busy shoppers she breezed through the front doors of *Chachee Couture*, the tiniest shop amongst the giants. She chuckled; if she blinked, she'd have missed it.

"*Bonjour.*" She waved to the salesgirl behind the counter on her way back to the fitting room. Once there, she meandered around mannequins in various modes of dress and tossed her bag onto a velvet settee.

"Ahh, *chéri*—" Chachee peered at her from behind a mannequin, his words becoming blunt. "You've lost weight."

"A few pounds." She grinned. "To better show off your creations?"

He waggled his finger and pointed beneath his eyes then at her.

"I ... uh ... couldn't sleep."

He tapped his foot, and called instructions to the seamstress, then glided out, shooting her a knowing look over his shoulder. An hour later, after Julia had been fitted, he waltzed back to view the result.

"Ravishing, *chéri*." He studied her beneath his pierced brows, angling his head this way and that. "Lose the sash." Nodding, he twirled his hand in the air. "A romantic, sexy look is what we're after."

"So, is this a big show?" Julia stood still while the seamstress made the changes.

"A matter of perspective." He turned his attention to the new designs on the art-board, his vague answer unsettling.

"Chachee?"

"*Bien.*" He swung away from handling the fabric samples draped over the rack and faced her. "An exclusive, *chéri*."

She balked. "You know I don't do private shows."

He nodded, twisting the ruby ring on his forefinger. "I wish you'd reconsider this one."

"Why?"

He shrugged. "Doesn't matter, forget I mentioned it."

"Something's wrong," she said. "What is it, Chach?"

"*Rien* … nothing."

"Look me in the eye and say that."

He did. "I'm strapped for cash for the fall collection, and this gig could turn it around, if—" Breaking off, he looked at her with his limpid brown eyes and gestured upward with his palms. "Sorry, *chéri*. I'm asking too much of you."

"Guilt tripping me, Chachee?" Julia nodded but it was underlined with a smile.

"*Bon!*" He grabbed her by the waist and twirled her around before setting her on her feet, to the seamstress' clicking tongue. "The guy wants to buy an original for his wife … a surprise." Excitement lit up his face, and left Julia speechless. "A private showing would ensure it's kept under wraps. No fashion press, no media sharks."

"So, get another model," she quipped.

"You're the best I've got."

"Since when?"

He chuckled, dismissing her query with a flick of his hand. "The ultra-rich are sooo eccentric," he mused. "In exchange for strutting your stuff, he'll dish out an obscene amount of cash."

"A little odd …" Oh, heck, how could she say no? She owed him for helping her in the past, and he was calling her on it. Besides, the extra cash would help with legal fees. "Better be on the level, Chach."

"A dresser, hairstylist and makeup artist will be with you."

Shaking her head, she laughed. "Very well."

"You won't regret it." He took her fingertips and waltzed her around before handing her over to the seamstress. "We'll celebrate afterward."

"About?"

"Er … the fall fashion line." His grin turned into a laugh. "Life, love … everything."

In the guest dressing room of the penthouse suite at the Hilton Arc de Triomphe Paris Hotel, Julia stood gazing out the wide expanse of window at *La Ville Lumière* … the City of Lights, Paris.

The Eiffel Tower glittered, and far below, cars looked like toys traveling along the Champs-Élysées, the most beautiful avenue in the world. Further, riverboats cruising the Seine sparkled with lanterns; during the day artists parked along its banks, painting their creations.

Julia wiggled into the sleek sapphire gown, and her dresser zipped her up, smoothing the chiffon flaring at her ankles. The off-the-shoulder neckline was both demure and sexy, allowing for only a glimpse of cleavage.

"A touch of mystery," Chachee had told his girls, "is so much more alluring than letting it all hang out."

And that of course had them bursting out laughing. A hint of a smile brushed her mouth at the thought. Wise Chachee.

"*Belle*," the hairstylist gushed, clipping her hair to the side, and keeping it trailing down her back.

"You forgot to spray my locks." Julia spun around, making a funny face at them in jest, and the gold threads jingled at her earlobes.

"Not for this showing," the hairstylist said, beginning to pack her things.

"*Au naturelle* for tonight." The make-up artist buffed her nose with the lightest of powder and nodded to the dresser.

"No stage lights to wash me out." Julia chuckled, slipping her feet into slinky gold stilettos. "Makes sense."

"You're ready, *mademoiselle*." The dresser walked across the room and opened the adjoining door. Julia shook her moist hands and took a step toward the open door. A pause, a breath, and she put her game-face on. *Voila*! The mannequin—every man's fantasy. She stepped across the threshold, heard the door click behind her and just for a second, a frisson of uncertainty zapped her. Wiggling her shoulders, she shook it off and strolled across the spacious living room and through the French doors to the wrap-around garden terrace overlooking the spectacular view of Paris.

Nobody was there.

She muffled a nervous giggle with her hand, and the diamond-studded gold bracelet jangled at her wrist. Shrugging, she placed her hand on her hip and sauntered across to the rail, making a perfected pose beneath the single lit lamp. She'd wait five minutes max and if the guy was a no-show, she'd get the heck outta there. In the meantime, she scanned the area beneath her mascara-laden lashes.

A table for two, a champagne bottle on ice, candles, and a mouthwatering aroma floated to her from somewhere in the suite. A portable electric fireplace blazed nearby. Mmm, it was a nice touch.

Her stomach gurgled. She'd only grabbed a glass of orange juice on her way out that morning, and she was famished. But she'd have to wait until she got home before eating, and hope her stomach didn't go into sound-effects mode again.

"Hmm, what gives?" she murmured. Boy oh boy, when she got her hands on Chachee, she'd give him a tongue-lashing. "Where is the mystery man?"

"Right here, Julia."

She spun around, and her mouth nearly hung open. "Mario." The momentum made her teeter on her stilettos, and she hugged the post behind her for support. "What are you doing here?"

"Buying a gown for my wife." He flashed her a broad grin. "Our one-year anniversary."

"O-okay." With a bemused smile on her lips, she pushed away from the lamppost, strutted across the patio and twirled around. "Will this do?"

"Yes. I'll take the gown."

"And I'll take the model." Another man stepped from the shadows. "For the night."

"No." She stumbled back a step and clutched the chrome back of a chair, her heart thudding. The lamplight cast shadows on his face, making him appear sinister, but she'd know him, his voice, and his presence anywhere.

"Yes," he shot back, his tone smooth steel.

"Michalis." His name a breath of sound from her mouth, then she infused wry humor in her words. "What brings you here?"

"Unfinished business."

"You set me up." She glanced at Mario, but he avoided direct eye contact. "The show, the gown, the wife … all a con?"

"On the contrary, my love," Michalis bit back. "You've mastered the sleight of hand, having managed to disappear from under my nose twice."

"Chachee" —she glanced away, her voice quivering— "was in on this?"

"I'm sorry, Jul—" Mario began, but Michalis held up a hand, nixing his apology.

A knife twisted in her breast. This certainly was not a case of distance making the heart grow fonder, but by the glacial glint in Michalis' eyes, the antithesis, breeding contempt.

"Don't blame him too much," Michalis said. "Chachee was doing it for a good cause."

She snapped her head around.

"The newlyweds." He set his mouth in a hard line, the skin on his cheeks stretching thin, his features more hawkish. "Mario and—"

"Michalis' sister," Mario added, the grin broadening on his face. "Maria."

"Ahh, what?" The query burst from her mouth, and her knuckles gleamed white on the chair. "Nanny Maria?"

Mario nodded, pleased. "My sweet ex-novitiate."

115

"You're not serious."

"I am." Mario crossed his heart with his forefinger.

"A novitiate?" Julia shot Michalis a lethal look. "In a sexy negligee, tottering from the bedroom into your arms?" A whoop of sound burst from deep in her throat. "I don't think so."

"She'd just left the Order and—" began Mario, but Michalis nabbed the words from his mouth.

"She'd been opening the gifts her cousins had given her for their honeymoon."

If Julia concentrated real hard, she'd ferret out the funny side to all this, but for the life of her, she couldn't find it. "I don't understand. How? When?" Questions crowded on her tongue, ready to tumble out, but she held them in check, as the colossal blunder she'd committed rocked her. "I-I didn't know you were married, Mario,"

"And to 'the other woman' no less," Michalis fired his shot, right into her heart, his mouth twisting in derision.

"I-I didn't know," she repeated, feeling about two inches high.

"That's because you jetted out of the zone without saying goodbye."

His sarcasm chafed her skin to the raw, and she struck back, her words targeting the bull's eye.

"You knew your sister was getting married, and you didn't tell me?" She shook her head to clear it and stood to her full height of five foot eight inches, but with her stilettos, she almost matched his six-foot height, and speared him with a clear look. "Didn't even tell me you had a sister?"

"I intended to," he muttered. "But it got complicated—"

"My fault." Maria stood behind them, cleared her throat and delivered her bombshell.

"No." Michalis was quick to interject.

"Yes, Michalis," she insisted, fingering the white apron covering her purple shift. "You've taken care of me all these years, and now I have to do my part." She gave Julia a faint smile. "Everything was happening at once ... my release from the convent, meeting Mario, my upcoming marriage ... finding out I had a sister-in-law." A huff of a breath, and her tone turned apologetic. "Overwhelmed, I'd asked Michalis to let me get used to the sudden changes in my life before—"

"Meeting me," Julia murmured. "Another change in your 'world.'"

Maria nodded, her brown curls bobbing. "Both excited and scared, I'd rushed to Michalis that day to meet you—" Her words cracked, and she swallowed. "Then, you walked in on us a-and—"

Flat out floored would hardly describe how Julia was feeling at this moment.

"I felt so guilty ... your break-up ... confused ..." She rubbed her hands over her arms, and peered at Mario beneath her lashes. "Life in the convent or life with Mario?"

"Maria ..." Mario interjected, seeing the anguish on her face. "We get it. You don't have to go on."

"Yes, I do." She stepped closer, glancing from one to the other before her gaze settled on Julia. "So I ran away," she confessed. "Back to the convent, and stayed in seclusion for a month, praying for an answer."

Such silence, one could have heard a pin drop. Julia dared not breathe, let alone utter a word.

"Mother Superior helped me understand my true calling." She heaved a deep sigh. "I had to go where God led me ..." she blinked tears trembling on her lashes. "And He led me to Mario."

Mario opened his arms and she ran to him, a nervous hiccup muffled against his vest. "Am I making sense to anyone?"

A rhetorical question of course, but it left Julia wanting to sink through the floor and be washed out to the River Seine.

"But surely ..." she thought aloud, allowing her words to drift. "You wore no rings."

"At the jewelers being reset for our anniversary," Mario

117

confessed, not fazing her fury toward one tall Greek shipping magnate.

Julia drew in a sharp breath, certain her displeasure was reflected in her eyes, now clashing with Michalis'. "You had a year to set things right …" She crinkled her brow "… and these last few days you could've explained, but …"

"As we were parting company," he said, his tone indifferent, "there was no need for explanations."

She squinted at him, shock waves rocking her, and realized it was more than that. Much more.

She and Michalis were locked in a tug-o-war of wills.

His pride … her defiance.

And something far beyond that but she couldn't quite tag it yet.

Reading the signals, Maria disengaged herself from Mario's embrace, and mumbling something about dessert, scuttled back inside. Mario extracted a lighter from the pocket of his *maitre'd* uniform, lit the candles on the table and retreated into the suite.

"I see," Julia murmured, collapsing in the chair.

"I doubt it," Michalis muttered, a brooding look on his face.

A romantic melody floated to them from inside the living room, and she cringed. Hardly subtle. Laughter bubbled from her, the sound grating in the already volatile atmosphere between them.

Taciturn, Michalis scowled.

Could she really blame him? Every time he'd tried to reach out to her these last few days in Greece, she'd snubbed him. And then, his big ego kicked in and here they were at another impasse; the other two in the kitchen trying to set up a romantic rendez-vous for them. Her shoulders shook with the humor of it, and she hiccupped. Not funny.

"I find nothing amusing here, Julia."

She nodded. "Of course not."

Her life was going down the drain, and she didn't know what

118

to do about it. Except maybe, start by delving into her own doubts, and where they'd flared.

A crescendo of sound in the background, and she straightened in her chair. Lolita.

The pieces were clicking in place. How could a man like Michalis love her? Her mother's abandonment proved she didn't deserve to be loved, didn't it? Julia flinched. Her past fear of being abandoned had sabotaged her future with Michalis at the first test.

She fidgeted in her seat and interlocked her fingers beneath the table.

A sliver of air diffused between her teeth, and Michalis caught the sound, his pointed gaze harpooning into her. A raw ache throbbed inside her. She couldn't fault her childhood or her mom's way of life on how things had turned out between her and Michalis. She was responsible for her decisions. She rubbed her hands over her arms, calming the goosebumps … not from chill in the air but from the ice-front blowing from Michalis.

She'd made a doozy of a *faux pas* where he was concerned. It had not only cost her a year of heartache and Amy not knowing her father but it had almost cost her sister-in-law's happiness.

"I-I'd like … to explain." A blush sheathed her body, and a shiver slid down her spine. The blush reflected her embarrassment, and the shiver because Michalis Leonadis was not a man who forgave easily. Her stunt had cost him three months of his daughter's life, not to mention mega bucks and their high-profile break-up splashed on every media outlet.

A foreboding silence ensued, except for the whirring of a helicopter above them.

She could very well be too late in her attempt to make amends for her foolhardiness.

His next words jotted a period at the end of her assumption.

"A little late in the game for that, Julia. It changes nothing."

Heartless boor, but she kept her choice words to herself.

He studied her beneath his aristocratic brow. "However, we still have business to discuss where my daughter's concerned."

Her heart sank like a stone. Nothing would put a dent in his male armor.

"We-e do." She nodded her assent, perspiration breaking out from her every pore, a trickle between her breasts. If she could just flee the scene … flee Michalis … flee the past, the present, and get some semblance of order in her life. Of course, he'd have none of that.

He wanted retribution.

A shockwave jolted through her. And he'd get it. On his terms. That much she knew about the man she'd married.

Her recent escape from Athens had simply compounded the situation between them. Her shoulders sagged. He held all the cards.

Except one.

In the background, the last chord of the song rang out, bringing a hint of a smile to her stiff lips, and with it a glimmer of light in the darkness. He held the deck, but she had the prize he wanted above all. Amy.

Perhaps she could still turn the tables on her husband. Amy deserved the parents that she and Michalis had never had. She'd fight for her daughter and for herself. As much as she denied it, he still left her breathless, her heart yearning for him.

"Of course, you're right," she whispered. He might be geared up to punish her for her past deeds, but she intended to take a swing or two of her own. She bit the quiver from her lip. "We must put an end to this."

His eyes shuttered.

"Perhaps a poor choice of words," she murmured, but he didn't take the bait.

"Not at all." He adjusted the collar of his jacket and snapped the sleeves in place, muting the glint of diamond cufflinks beneath. "Couldn't have put it better myself."

She nodded, absently fingering the empty champagne flute. "Now, shall we dine?"

"I'm not hungry." She leaped to her feet, and her stomach growled. Mortified, she sank back down. "Well, maybe a little."

"Good." He chuckled, the sound humorless. "I've had a long flight, and I am hungry." Pulling out a chair, he sat down beside her, so close his thigh grazed hers, his heat slipping into her, alerting her vitals. "You'll think more clearly after you've eaten."

"I'm thinking clearly now," she batted back, tightening her grip on the stem of the champagne flute.

His arched brow spoke volumes.

"Crystal clear," she insisted. His overpowering presence had her shifting in her chair, but his magnetism entrapped her to the spot.

She cast him a veiled glance beneath her lashes, her breath bouncing in her chest, her nerves bopping. The designer threads he wore with such ease made him look so debonair and sexy, she almost raised her hand to fan her feverish face, but exerted extreme self-control. She couldn't miss a beat where Michalis was concerned; not when there was so much at stake.

"If you insist," he said, but didn't elaborate.

An aura of such masculinity emanated from him, triggering erotic sensations inside her, she wondered how she'd make it through the evening.

Not a good sign for her. Maybe if she clobbered him with the warming platter lid—she muffled a giggle. Nope. Not a good idea either.

"Something funny?" he asked, reaching for the champagne bottle.

"Not at all."

"You still owe me, fantasy girl," he ground out, wiping the hint of humor from her mouth. "A month's worth, but we'll start with tonight."

"Twenty-four days."

"Still counting."

"What if I am?" She tilted her chin in defiance, but her bravado didn't faze him. Rather it stacked against her.

"It's twenty-seven," he clipped, giving her no quarter. "The three days you ditched don't count."

Suddenly feeling light headed, she laughed, the sound drifting above the melody in the background. "This is crazy."

"Actually, it's good business sense."

"Is everything business with you?"

He paused, his hand around the bottleneck, his eyes examining every nuance on her face before dipping to her cleavage. A heartbeat, and his gaze bounced back to her eyes, drilling into her and jarring every nerve in her body. "Not everything."

She drew in a sharp breath, chafing her throat, and dropped her hands in her lap, folding her fingers into fists.

"Business and pleasure works for me." He popped the cork and the golden liquid foamed, fueling the air with the delicate scent of champagne. "A combo deal."

"Well, it doesn't for me."

He cocked his head, a killer smile on his mouth. "There must be a way to change your mind."

"Fat chance, Michalis."

"Mega bucks" —he inclined his head to the manila envelope on the coffee table inside the suite— "seem to do the trick."

"F-fine." She clamped down on the hysteria on the brink of bubbling from her. It was what she wanted for her daughter, a secure future. And then annoyance fizzed inside her, and she went one better. "Before or after dinner?"

"Definitely after."

How could she feel devastatingly attracted to him when he brought out the worst in her? She raised her chin, her bravado a screen, offsetting her reaction to his potent sensuality. "Why this farce, Michalis?" But he also brought out the best in her. Somewhere from deep in her memory, the thought flared to the

122

forefront, but she bashed it down. Any positives on him would weaken her resolve to banish him into her murky past as soon as possible. "Surely there's no need for this cat and mouse game."

"I'm a man of my word—" He filled her glass with champagne and then filled his own, the bubbles fizzing in the lull between his words.

She snorted, and gripped the flute, taking a long drink before setting it on the table. So much for her good intentions to take only a sip or two.

"Another?" He pursed his lips, considering her, and poised the bottle above her glass.

She covered the glass with her hand. "No." Not on an empty stomach, and besides, she needed her wits about her. "This is nonsense."

"You think discussing what's best for our child—"

Her hand flew to her temple, her head buzzing. "I don't want anything of yours."

He paled beneath his austere features. "Does that include Amy?"

"No!"

"Don't sound so shocked." He plunged the bottle into the ice bucket, and the crunch of ice grated on her nerves. "She's got my DNA too."

"You can't have her."

"Then you had better be willing to entertain me for the evening."

"Oh, let's get it over with." She made to stand, reaching for the zipper of her dress, but the hem of her gown snagged on the chair leg, and she had to plunk back down or rip the material.

"Here let me." He slid off his chair, got on one knee and reached to unravel the material.

"Michalis, there's no need—" Michalis, chivalrous? Her heart jolted. Much better for him to be the ogre so that she could shield her vulnerable emotions for him.

Moonlight glinted on his hair, and she wanted … almost reached out to touch, feel … him. Instead she curled her fingers, her fingernails digging into her palms, and pressed her lips together before she said something revealing.

"There that should do it."

"Thanks," she said between her teeth. "Bu-ut I really have to be going." Just then her stomach rumbled, and she slapped her hand on her abdomen to mute the revealing sound.

"Indulge me." Amusement tugged the corner of his mouth. "Eat first."

"Why?"

"Let's just say it's a farewell of sorts."

His words gouged a hole inside her, but she pinned a smile on her face, determined to hold her own with this man who had her heart throbbing for him. "What a way to go."

"On a full stomach?" he joked, lifting a lid from one of the serving platters, and the most delicious aroma reached her.

"Oh yum." She pinched a potato drenched in olive oil and sprinkled with oregano from the platter and placed it in her mouth. "Delish." She rolled her eyes in appreciation, provoking him. "I loooove Greek food."

"And is Greek food all you love?"

"Why Michalis" —she grinned, her cheek bulging with food, chewed and swallowed— "that's a leading question." She licked her mouth, then her index finger and thumb, noting his grip tightening on his fork. Good, she'd gotten a reaction, even if it was ever so subtle, and she found that immensely pleasing.

"To which you no doubt have a ready answer."

The air crackled with combustible ions pulsing between them. A misstep, and she'd be incinerated. For self-preservation, she upped the ante by calling his shot. "I do, if I cared to give it."

"Perhaps before the night is over, you won't have any trouble voicing it, hmm?"

Drat the man; he always managed to get the upper hand in

any discourse. If she had to go through this farce with him tonight, at least in the morning, she could literarily kiss Michalis Leonadis goodbye.

A stitch of such intense longing assailed her senses, and for a second fogged up her common sense. Except for Amy linking them, she'd have to sever all ties with him in order to go on with her life. Her heart splintered. Every time she looked at her daughter, she'd be crushed, seeing Michalis reflected in her eyes.

"Maria's a good cook," she tossed out of left field, needing to change the direction of her thoughts.

"Mmm, she is." Michalis reached for the glass of champagne and bringing it to his lips, looked at her over the rim. The crease between her brows cueing of an inner struggle she tried to knock off with her witty repartee ... and provoking him. Of course, that irked him the more. He downed half the drink in one go, set the glass back on the table, his jaw iron-hard. Julia Armstrong Leonadis owed him, big time. And so, a lesson she'd learn this night in his arms.

Sure it's not you, Mr. Hotshot who'll learn? His mind niggled. *It could backfire.* But he demolished the darts with his next words. "What's it to be, Julia?"

"Why, whatever do you mean?" She cast him a coy glance beneath her lashes, and that had him tightening his abs.

"There's a lot to sample." He picked up the serving spatula and plunged it in the dish of roast lamb. "What's your pleasure, Julia?" A wicked grin played on his mouth. "We're bound to be here all night."

"Well then, serve up, Michalis." She smiled, dimpling her cheek, and that booted him smack center of his gut. "I'm ready to eat."

"All in good time," he said, his voice deepening. "Slow 'n easy, is how it's going to be."

Chapter 12

"Well, then—" She peered at him from beneath her lashes, under-scoring his innuendos with her own ... just to aggravate him. "—hadn't we better warm-up with the first course?"

"You think we'll need a warm-up session?" He forked a slice of roast lamb and placed it on her plate, nixing her provocative words with his wisecrack.

"Not we ... you." Overly sweetly, she batted it out of the park, and had him crunching nails beneath his molars. "Thought you might be a little rusty." She picked up her glass, her eyes steady on his face, then a downward sweep of her lashes, and she took a sip of the bubbly.

Control, Leonadis ... and charm, man.

He winked. "You'll have to show me the moves then, won't you?"

The wine spurted from her mouth.

"It's okay." He held out his napkin to her. "I'm a quick study."

"I can just imagine."

"Sounds like a yes to me." A pause and, "Salad?" He offered her the bowl of Greek salad, and when she didn't answer, scooped some on her plate. "But it'll be on my time and my call, fantasy girl."

"That's no surprise, Michalis." Snatching up her knife and fork, she decimated the food on her plate, and then realizing what she'd done, stopped, the knife and fork hovering in midair. The disbelieving look on her face made the amusement humming in his throat morph into a full-fledged laugh.

"You going to eat that mush, now?"

"Maybe, maybe not." She twirled the food around on the plate with her fork and cleared her throat. "Why don't we just call" —she waved a hand around at the romantic setup— "all this off?" Then, she softened her voice to a purr, sexy as all heck. "You have nothing to prove … to me."

"But perhaps you have something to prove to me," he said, batting a homerun, but his gut hitched.

She laughed; the sound soft and clear activated his senses.

"I do not."

"Time will tell the tale, no?"

"Can we be adults about this, Michalis?"

"We're not?"

"We know where we stand—"

"Do we?"

"Surely, there's no need for the seduction scene," she murmured, ignoring his question. "This dinner, the music—"

"Not my idea, but—" He shrugged, inclining his head toward the kitchen. "Don't want to disappoint them, do we?"

She reluctantly shook her head.

"Good." He pierced an olive with a toothpick and held it to her mouth. "Open up, they might be watching."

She did. He placed the olive on her tongue, and she snapped her teeth, barely missing his fingers.

"Easy now." He shook his fingers, watching her pulverize the olive in her mouth. "Has a bite to it, mmm?" The pun sounded from deep in his throat, and with it a shift closer to the inevitable.

For his trouble, he got caught in the crossfire of the green sparks shooting from her eyes, but just for a second. He ducked, pouncing on the food in his plate and then pointed his fork at her plate. "Now, eat up, you'll need your strength."

She seemed to pale, but that could be an illusion of the lamp-light shining on her face. Without another word, she set the utensils down, picked up the linen napkin and dropped it on her lap.

Leonadis you're pushing the caveman tactics, the warning nicked his mind, but he doused it by chowing down on a lamb chop.

She shot him a look that would frazzle a lesser man, and he eclipsed it by raising his glass.

"A toast."

A long pause, a tilt of her head, and circling the stem with her fingers, she lifted the flute, her mouth a straight line. She waited, and that irritated the heck out of him. She wasn't helping. Not giving an inch, or a word.

He clinked her glass with his and cleared his throat. "To an unforgettable evening."

"New beginnings ..." she murmured, the words trailing away.

He brought the glass to his mouth, paused, his steady gaze on her face for any hint that she was thawing. A sound close to a growl from his throat, then he tipped the glass, gulping the golden liquid in one go. He smacked his lips. "A good vintage."

Julia took a sip, the effervescence tickling her nose, and the wine sliding down her throat, warmed her insides. Their earlier banter had her hoping he'd see sense, but determined to collect his due, he left her no choice but to do her utmost to thwart his agenda.

A tug-o-war would surely ensue between them ... had already begun.

Setting the glass down, she picked up her fork and went through the motions of eating, frustrating his attempt at conver-sation with one word replies. Finally, except for the clink of cutlery on the china and the romantic tunes still floating about, silence enveloped them.

Time crawled by, and she barely remembered what she'd tasted, for certainly she hadn't eaten much. She set her fork down, annoyance zinging through her; she both anticipated and dreaded what was on the evening's agenda. What was the matter with her?

"You've barely touched your food."

Well, he'd noticed, and that was something in her favor, she smirked.

He set his cutlery down, picked up the napkin and blotted his mouth. "Something wrong?"

A beat, and he snapped his fingers, preempting her tart reply before she could voice it. Mario stepped from the shadows, a white napkin over his forearm and a flaming dish in his hands.

She rolled her eyes. "What's this?"

"Cherries Jubilee." Maria stepped out carrying a tray with two demitasses of Greek coffee and walking ahead of Mario, put the cups on the table. Stacking the used dishes on the tray, she cleared space and Mario set the decadent dessert between them. "So out-of-this-world good."

"Impeccable service, Mario … Maria," Michalis murmured.

Maria scurried back inside, and a second later Mario followed her.

"My compliments," Michalis said, handing her a spoon.

Was this intimate overture … sharing this delectable dessert with him the shift in the program for the night? While she thought it out, he'd scooped up a spoonful and brought it to her mouth.

"Thanks." She took the offering, the tangy-sweet concoction sliding over her tongue and stimulating her taste buds.

"That wasn't so bad, was it?" He reached out and flicked the drip of syrup from the corner of her mouth, then licked his thumb. "Mmm, good."

"It is." She chewed and swallowed. "Aren't you going to have any?"

"I did." He picked up his cup, took a gulp of the brew, his

eyes level on her face … her mouth … his meaning unmistakable.

Julia snatched up her napkin, blotted her lip and picking up the demitasse, took a sip of the bittersweet brew.

A reflection of her life.

"Julia …"

"Michalis …"

They spoke in unison, and then his chuckle and her giggle merged, diffusing the coiled tension.

He put his cup down, took hers from her hand and setting it down next to his, pushed his chair back and stood. "Come." Pulling her up into his arms, he waltzed her into the living room, halted at the coffee table and with her still in his embrace, swept up a velvet case on top of the manila envelope.

"Wha-at's this?" she murmured, her voice breaking.

"Shh." He placed two fingers on her lips. "This evening's a fantasy, remember?"

Yes, and fantasies end when you wake up in the morning, the thought battered her brain and scoured her heart raw.

He clicked the case open. She sucked in her breath, and her hand fluttered to her mouth. Turning her around, he lifted the necklace and encircling her throat with the diamonds, secured the clasp, his fingers feathering her nape.

A sting of heat shot into her, and she fingered a diamond nestling at her cleavage. Ice-cold yet hot as hellfire.

"I can't accept—"

"You can and you will, *agape mou.*" He curled his mouth in a cynical line. "For tonight."

"Michalis …" She reached out to him, to touch his arm, to put a stop to this madness, for surely that's all it could be.

He reached out for the silver-lamine stole on the sofa and wrapped it around her shoulders and just for a second felt the pressure of his fingers on her skin. "And to complete the fairytale, this." Seizing a matching evening bag, he plunked it in her hands, a tick at his temple.

"I-I," she began, but his set face stifled her words.

"Open it, Julia."

"This is silly." But she did open it and tottered back a step, the ring sparkling in the scarlet folds of the purse.

"Your wedding ring," he bit out, his mouth a hard line. "You'd left it behind, as you'd abandoned everything else."

"I-I ca-an't." She shook her head. "Please …"

"A prop for tonight's fantasy," he muttered, his sub-zero words icing her flesh. "Afterward, you can pawn it."

Before she could slam him with a response, he'd pulled out the gold circle, slid it on her finger and pressed his lips to the spot. His feather-light kiss had her insides swirling and a stake stabbing her heart, cutting off her air supply.

Tension vibrated, the silence seeming endless … even the music had stopped. Desire, anger, resentment, regret amalgamated in that minuscule slice of time, fueling the emotional time bomb ticking between them.

"Shall we go?" he said, his tone more a demand than a request … but his words caused the dynamics to shift, and she filled her lungs with oxygen.

"No." She exhaled the word, took a step back and rubbed her moist palms together. "I think this has gone far enough, Michalis."

A nerve ticked at the corner of his mouth, and his eyes shadowed.

"You've … made your point."

"And that is?"

"You can show a girl a good time?" About to buckle, she shot from the hip in an attempt to diffuse the high voltage crackling between them.

Bittersweet sensation lathered her insides, and she nearly did double over then, but gripped the back of the sofa, retaining her upright stance. "When will you stop—?"

He held up an imperious hand, nixing the words '—punishing

131

me?' on the tip of her tongue. "I've not yet begun to show you the fairytale, princess."

"You don't have to—"

"Oh, but I do." He stepped closer, cupping her chin, his thumb stroking the corner of her mouth, and sending a jolt of sensation smack into her center.

Had she not been so quick to condemn, she'd have known the family she so craved, she already had with him; her husband, her baby and her sister-in-law. A void gaped open inside her. He was still hell bent on revenge.

Was he flaunting it all before her, just to take it all away ... including Amy? She pinched the crease between her brows ... but Michalis wasn't the flamboyant type.

A hint of a smile curved her mouth, and he narrowed his gaze, his jaw taut.

On the contrary, he was direct to a fault, and unyielding when it suited him. Obviously, getting retribution for what she'd done to him suited him. Punish her? He'd never hurt her of course, but Michalis Leonadis would score his way.

She brushed the back of her hand across her brow, and licked her lips.

A grunt sounded from his side of the room, but she dismissed it.

"This is so unreal," she murmured beneath her breath, but he cocked his head, having heard.

She supposed it was no use dragging this vendetta out. The sooner the evening wrapped, the sooner she could get away from Michalis and mend her broken heart. Wry amusement scratched her throat at the trite sentiment, but she had to piece her life together again, if for no one else, then for Amy.

"True." He trailed his hand over her shoulder, down her arm to her palm and gripped her fingertips. "Come."

"Where?"

"A surprise."

"I-I don't know if I can handle any more of those."

A twitch at the corner of his mouth, but it went no further. "You'll like this one."

He escorted her into the suite's private elevator and they ascended to the rooftop helipad. The helicopter's rotor whipped the air, and he wedged her close to his side before making a dash against the current. He ushered her into the luxurious interior but not before she caught the ML insignia emblazoned across the door.

Speechless, Julia strapped herself into the passenger seat with Michalis next to her, so close his jacket sleeve brushed her elbow and sent tingles up her arm. She shifted in her seat and wrapped the stole closer about her shoulders.

"Ready for lift-off, Mr. Leonadis?"

Julia laughed, recognizing the voice. "Let me guess ..."

The pilot turned and grinned.

"Mario."

"At your service." He tapped two fingers to his cap, and resumed flicking switches on the control panel.

"A cocktail before we're airborne?" Another familiar voice sailed from behind them and Julia twisted around, blinking at Maria playing hostess onboard. "There's designer water, designer water and designer water." A giggle. "Various flavors and brands."

"No, thank y—" Nothing should surprise her where her husband was concerned. Her hand flew to her mouth. *Husband?* She'd elicited the word from somewhere in her subconscious, and a warmth curled up inside her. Silently she echoed the word in her head. Somehow it sounded, no, felt right. She pursed her lips, and rejected the thought. *Don't be a ninny*. Her pulse skittered, and she gripped the chair, her fingers pressing into the expensive upholstery.

Tonight was a detour on the road to the divorce court.

"Perrier on ice." Michalis placed his order, winked at Maria, and ignored Julia.

* * *

It was well past one in the morning when they returned from the Paris Opera House, and Michalis inserted the key-tab in the door of the penthouse suite. He shoved it open, and Julia made to pass him.

"Oh ho, no you don't." He scooped her up in his arms and crossed the threshold, the door slamming shut behind him.

Julia stilled in his arms. His breath caressed her cheek, his warmth seeping into her and stimulating every nerve ending. The subtle scent of his cologne filled her senses, and she wanted to snuggle closer, nuzzle his neck. Of course she did neither. Instead, she wiggled in his embrace, hiding her vulnerability, her words sounding shrewish even to her own ears. "Put me down."

"Sure thing." He dropped her on her feet so fast that she staggered a step, her hands spanning the wall for support. Sidestepping her, he flicked on a muted light, took off his jacket, tossed it on the sofa and loosened his tie. A pause, and he cupped her shoulders possessively, but a second later, he slid the wrap from her shoulders, placing it on the couch next to his jacket. "A nightcap?"

"What?" she asked, tongue-in-cheek. "No, Mario? Maria?"

He chuckled, heading to the bar. "Just me."

Chapter 13

Julia clutched the evening bag he'd given her and twisting the ring on her finger, she closed her eyes for a second, a bemused smile brushing her mouth.

It was a mirage, like the evening's entertainment, and yet, a sense of magic enfolded her.

Once they'd lifted off in the Leonadis helicopter, it had indeed been a fairyland ride with Paris all a-glitter below them. The enchanted evening continued with *The Magic Flute*, an opera tugging at the heart and flailing the emotions. And for a little while, lost in the storyline, Julia had forgotten her woes. But now she was back, and for some reason, the spell wrapped around her not letting go. Cloistered in the suite with Michalis, it could be dangerous to her psyche … her heart.

"Nice of Maria and Mario to take over from Mrs. Knightley and babysit Amy," she chit-chatted.

Michalis inclined his head. "Sherry?" he asked, setting two goblets and a decanter on the counter.

"Tea please." That would give her a semblance of reality, she thought, rubbing her arms with her hands.

"Tea?"

"If it's too much trouble—"

"No trouble." He led the way to the kitchen, and paused center floor, glancing this way and that. "Hmm, teabags ... where—"

"Can you boil water?"

"Of course." But he didn't move, a pained look on his features.

She laughed, and the tension inside her eased. Bypassing the micro-oven, she grabbed the kettle from the counter, filled it with water from the faucet—high tech stuff, she didn't even have to turn it on, just wave her hand beneath it—set it on the stove and pressed the on button to heat the element. When the water began to steam, she folded her arms across her bosom and tapped her toe on the tile, waiting for him to deliver.

"Uh ... right." He played along and hopped to it, rifling through drawers for the elusive teabags. Finally, he pulled his hand out of a drawer, clutching several teabags. "Got 'em!"

"Amazing."

He flashed her a killer smile, his cheek grooved in that elongated dimple ... and oh my, he looked so devastatingly handsome, her stomach jittered.

"What's your pleasure?" He fanned the packets with his fingers like playing cards. "Orange cinnamon, cherry zinger, passion fruit."

"Cherry."

Tossing the teabags on the counter, he flipped a couple of mugs from the cupboard, took her chosen teabag and opening it, dropped it in the cup.

"Aren't you going to have any?"

"Not my—" he began, and then changed his mind. "Passion sounds like a possibility."

A moment loaded with innuendo, but thankfully, the kettle whistled, and Julia twisted away from his searching gaze. Pressing the off button, she picked up the kettle and poured hot water into her mug. The soothing scent of cherry blossom filled the kitchen, and then she turned to fill his mug.

"Here let me." He reached to take the pot from her hand, but she spun away so abruptly, a drop of hot liquid splattered on her hand.

"Ohh," She jerked, dropping the kettle so quickly that it clattered on the counter, and she reached for the faucet. But Michalis was ahead of her, and taking her hand, placed it under the cold stream.

"It'll sting at first," he said, his tone gruff, making her wonder if there was a double meaning in his words. "But then it'll dull to a throb."

She'd been stung times a million when she'd left him—then, she caught herself up from recalling what was best forgotten. A wheeze of a breath, and a sliver of sound on exhale. "I'm tougher than I look." She'd had to be. Learned to be.

Must learn to be again.

He smiled, and had her pulse tripping. Crazy stuff, she mused, jitters skipping through her.

"As I'm fast discovering." When the water stopped gushing, he lifted her hand to his mouth and flicked his tongue over the injury. "Better?" he murmured, his breath a coolant upon her scalded skin.

"Much, thanks." She made to withdraw her hand from his grasp, but he continued his ministrations; a kiss on her palm then her fingers, before drawing each digit into his mouth. Then he blew upon each one, his breath tingling her skin, sending erotic impulses through her body, tightness in her breast.

"Michalis," she gasped, and he lifted his head, his mouth a hair-breadth from her lips.

Time stood still, and then his mouth crushed hers. His kiss was an explosion of desire, anger, exasperation, frustration and lust. For it couldn't be the other deeper emotion, could it? A whimper bumped its way from her throat to her mouth, but he lapped it up with his tongue.

She sagged against him, her breath mingling with his, and his tongue seduced her into a waltz of the senses. Banishing the fuzzy warning at the back of her mind, she joined him in the sensual dance to another tempo in her brain. One time, one last time with him, and she could close the chapter on Michalis Leonadis.

Wrong.

He wanted twenty-seven nights with her.

Well, the countdown would have to begin with night number one, wouldn't it? And with that thought, she curved in to him, wrapping her arms around his neck, her fingers weaving through his hair. This bittersweet interlude would have to last her a lifetime. The man she ... oh dear God ... she loved him, always would be a slave to her feelings for Michalis Leonadis.

That's why she had to 'pay up' and get the heck out of there.

He loved her not.

Otherwise, she'd be an emotionally challenged wretch, knowing he only wanted her to satisfy his lust for revenge. For their daughter's sake, she had to sever her personal ties with the only man who made her senses sing.

"Julia ..." he rasped her name deep in his throat, and reading her clear signal, swept her up in his arms.

"Michalis *mou* ..." She nuzzled his neck, her words muffled, her arms holding him tight.

He strode from the kitchen, crossed the living room, bumped into a settee, smothered an oath, his mouth smiling against hers, and marched into the bedroom, booting the door closed.

He set her on her feet, his hands spanning her waist, then gradually his fingers inched upward to the zipper. Slowly, he drew the zip down, the tips of his fingers igniting sparks of fire along her spine.

"Not fair," she mumbled into his neck.

"All's fair in ..." he breathed into her ear. Sliding his hand around her midriff, and upward, he cupped her breast.

Drawing a gasp from her, he drank the sound in with his mouth, his thumb dallying at her nipple. He slid his mouth along her jaw and lower, nuzzling her nape, his hand explored her abdomen, swerved beneath the loose material and palming her tush, pulled her smack against his arousal.

While he shimmied the gown over her hips, she unbuttoned his shirt, sliding her hands up his chest, then down, flicking his belly button, and tugging at his belt buckle.

An indrawn breath, and he covered her hand with his. "This way." He unbuckled his belt, and fell into her hands. "No going back," he panted into her bosom, his fingers creating a riot in her hair.

"I-I know," she breathed the words, stroking his length, her pulse deafening in her ears.

"In that case ..." He lifted her up, swung her around and tumbled on the bed with her. Joy bubbled from her in a nervous giggle, and he claimed it with his mouth, his hands holding her head steady for the sensual onslaught.

The air sizzled with sexual fervor.

His thumbs feathered the pulse points at her throat and his mouth inched that way, feasting on the erratic beat. He nibbled his way to the swell of her breast, tugging at one nipple with his teeth, then his tongue swirled on the shadowed peak, and he took it fully into his mouth.

A purr from deep in her throat, and she arched up into him, clutching his shoulders, her fingers pressing into his flesh. His hand flirted with her other breast, and then he straddled her, an erotic rhythm pulsing between them.

Desire looped in her belly, and she wrapped her arms around his neck, her hands lost in the curls at the nape of his neck, her mouth gliding across his jaw to his mouth. A hot beat, and his hand slid down her midriff to her abdomen, his mouth following with a flick of his tongue at her navel, his fingers inching lower to fondle the curls between her thighs.

"Julia, my hea—" But her moan of delight drowned out what he'd been about to confess, his fingers working their magic on her sleek moistness.

"Michalis, I lo—" He crushed her mouth in a telling kiss, smothering her confession, and shifting his body, he positioned himself above her.

As his tongue plundered her mouth, he plunged into her, pulled back and drove deeper and higher inside her, matching the frenzied rhythm in her mouth. She wrapped her legs around him, drawing him in, her fingernails raking across his shoulder blades.

"Julia, *agape mou* ..." he panted, with each thrust.

"Michalis *mou*," she gasped into his mouth. Spasms rocked her body, coiled and burst in a flare of sensation inside; a second later he got his release, and slumped against her.

He cherished her in his arms, her body curved close to his, her head upon his heart, her hair splayed across his chest. "Time out, my love," he murmured. As he brushed back moist curls at her temple, he lay claim to the spot with his lips and drew the covers over them.

Fluttering her lashes closed, Julia dozed, but after what seemed like moments, she was aroused, a smile curving her mouth. His leg stroked against hers and awakened her senses anew. She stirred, taking him into her arms, into her heart and into her body.

An explosion of sexuality ... sounds, scents and sensual delight.

He made love to her over and over, until dawn invaded with a sliver of light against the curtains.

"Sweet dreams, my darling." He caressed her cheek with his fingers, a fleeting kiss, his words drifting to her, but she was too drowsy to make sense of them.

Exhausted, she burrowed under the covers, a smile on her mouth, and slept in the arms of the man she loved, the man she married ... the man of her dreams.

* * *

A sunbeam played fickle with her eyelids, and Julia fluttered her lashes open, the smile still plastered to her mouth. Feeling like she hadn't a care in the world, she stretched her limbs and her body hummed, although a little sore. The pleasure and the pain, she mused. She'd had both, and she much preferred the passion with her one and only love.

"Michalis *mou*," she breathed his name and reached out for him.

But her hand brushed the vacant space next to her.

Slowly she turned, and numbness crawled upward from her toes, stiffening her muscles in ice. Her heart pounded and her pulse leaped into her throat. He'd tossed the rumpled sheets aside on his side of the bed, and the note on the manila envelope propped up on his scrunched pillow, glared her in the face.

"Sleep in. Order breakfast. Check out 3 p.m." The line beneath his scrawled initials delivered the final blow. 'P.S. Paid in full, *agape mou.*'

She should be thankful he'd left after the one night. Obviously, he'd changed his mind about the other twenty-six. She started to shake and clutched the sheets between her nerveless fingers. "You bast—" but the moan blasting from deep inside her, stifled her choice words.

She felt gutted. His scent still lingered on the sheets, a bitter reminder of her folly. She curled beneath the covers, tears welling up in her eyes and flowing down her cheeks, soaking her pillow. Moments dragged on, and although her tears eased some of the numbness from her body, it only made the ache more acute. A heave of a breath, then another, and swatting her damp cheeks with the back of her hands, she peeked at the clock on the bedside stand.

Twelve-noon.

He must've skipped out hours ago while she was still in La La Land.

A whimper, and she flipped on her back, threw her arm over

her eyes, and tried to ignore the hollow in her stomach. With every fiber in her body aching, she pushed herself up on one elbow and snatched the envelope from his pillow. She drummed her fingers on the mattress and then socked the pillow, sending it flying across the room.

"Okay." She felt better for a second, then a moan whipped through her, belying that idea. Scooting up, she leaned against the headboard, pushed the hair off her face with a quivery hand and tore open the envelope.

She scanned the contents, the signature, the date, and slumped against the pillows, blood seeming to drain from her every cell.

Through a blur of tears she acknowledged the trust fund for Amy was intact as he'd promised. But she blinked and blinked some more at the other document with her name emblazoned on it. How could this be?

Julia Armstrong named Lolita Armstrong's beneficiary of fifty percent ownership in the Leonadis Boat Rentals and future assets from the business, now known as Leonadis International Cruise Line.

Tremors shook her body, and a whimper sounded from deep inside her. It had been her mother. Her mercenary mother that still haunted her.

Julia's temples pounded. Heaving a quivery breath, she reread the document that made her half owner of the Leonadis' billions. She keeled over on her side and giggled. The giggles grew to a hysterical pitch that made her eyes well up with new tears.

"I'm not poor." She tossed the papers in the air and they fluttered around her, landing on the blankets. "I'm rich."

She had an obscene amount of money, Michalis' money. She sniffed, hiccupped, and swatted the tears from her cheeks; then realization had her nerves twittering.

And all because of her scheming mother; who had just given Julia the ammo to battle Michalis for her daughter. She didn't know yet how her mother had pulled it off, but she could now fight Michalis, and with his own money.

Justice?

"Nope." She dragged herself from the bed and stood in the center of the room, her legs nearly buckling beneath her. A cry, almost a whine vibrated in her throat. She pressed her hand to her mouth. Fear stemming from her past and imbedded in her psyche, snaked around her and immobilized her.

Was she a replica of her mother?

She wobbled and gripped the bedpost. Then the truth smacked her right in the chest, knocked the breath from her, and she collapsed onto the carpet.

It wasn't Michalis. It was her, Julia; she had to make the choice, had to prove—

What had she done? Destroyed?

A knock sounded through the fog in her mind, and her heart lifted just for a second, until she realized Michalis wouldn't knock; he had a key to let himself in.

"Ju-ust a minute." She pushed herself up, grabbed a bathrobe from the bathroom and tying the sash around her waist, tottered to the door. "Coming."

She flung the door open and clung onto the door handle, her knuckles whitening. "Ma-ria, what're you doing here?" Then her words turned frantic. "Where's my daughter?"

Maria grinned. "My beautiful niece is with her uncle."

"Mario?" Her eyes narrowed. "Where?"

"Your pad."

At her words, relief soared through Julia. "I have to get to her." Guilt gnawed at her. "She needs me."

"Amy's having a blast with her Uncle Mario." A giggle, then she squinted at her more closely, and the giggle dissipated in her throat. "By the looks of you—"

"What brings you here so early?" Julia nipped her words and backed away, still too raw for discerning eyes.

Maria lifted a shapely brow, tapped her wristwatch, but made no further reference to the time of day. A lift of her shoulder, and she strolled inside closing the door behind her. "Forgot to give you an invite to our anniversary party, last night."

"Last night." Julia teetered, the words skimming her numb lips, and Maria leaped for her before she crumpled to the floor.

"Something is wrong." Maria helped her to the sofa and scanned the place. "Where's that stubborn brother of mine?"

Julia pressed her fingers to her mouth, her eyes brimming with tears.

"Tea?" Maria offered the quick remedy.

"Ye-es, please."

Chapter 14

"The man deserved a tongue lashing," Julia muttered beneath her breath, traipsing along the beach of Mermaid's Grotto. "Obviously—ouch!" She bumped her toe against a log of driftwood, her irate soliloquy disrupted. "'Paid in full', *agape mou*," Julia mimicked, rubbing her toe and clutching the manila envelope tighter in her hand. "Huh! Hardly."

Why else put her through this?

She shaded her eyes with her hand and squinted out to sea, still glimmering in the waning sunlight. And why was she going along with it? A rip of angst, then her stomach clenched. She had to confront him on this. Wanted to come clean ... wanted him to ... Gut-spilling time.

A tremor tore through her, her shoulders drooped, and she almost backtracked.

It hadn't taken Maria long to catch on; with the tea came talk, then a quick call to Mario—the shadowed figure in the photo of Maria and Michalis that Julia had despaired over on the yacht. And here she was now, about to face-off with Michalis.

If Michalis hadn't delivered the document, she'd never have known she owned half of the global giant. Why had he done it? To get rid of her? Or to soothe his conscience?

"I'll go, you stubborn Greek." Julia slapped the rolled up envelope in her hand, wishing she could swat Michalis with it. "But when I'm good and ready." Emboldened by her mutterings, she trudged on ready to do battle with one Michalis Leonadis.

A few yards further, she turned around an outcrop of barnacle-encrusted boulders, and saw him. She sagged against a flat rock, her heartbeat suspended for a second before thudding at super-sonic speed.

Bare-chested and with his trousers rolled up, he stood knee-deep in the water and tossed in a fishing line. The muscles of his back contracted and a glaze of sweat glinted on his shoulders. Not daring to move yet, she remained in the shelter of the rocks, a puff of sea breeze cooling her sun-kissed face.

A wayward sunbeam crowned him, adding flecks of gold to his hair, and for a moment it became so bright, she couldn't see him. The ray dipped beneath the horizon, and she spotlighted him. He was more devastating half-dressed in his roguish casuals with the surf crashing around him than in his sophisticated urban threads.

She glanced up at the sky streaked with color, then back at him, air filtering from her mouth in a shaky stream. Michalis Leonadis, a man of both worlds, a man who could sit with peas-ants and kings. The man she'd married for better or worse. Dare she hope the best was still possible for them? She'd been such a fool to believe the worst of him instead of—

He glanced her way, spotted her in his laser-beam focus, and then ignored her. This was not going to be easy, but guess she owed him this one. She walked closer, the sand squishing between her toes, the foam of the waves washing over her feet, and stopped several yards from him. A fresh dose of ocean air filled her lungs, the sea-tang making her cheeks tingle and reviving her after her flight from Paris in the Leonadis jet.

"Michalis." She waded in, until she stood beside him, the water rippling around her knees.

He reeled in his catch …

Her.

"Why didn't you tell me?" she accused. "You had the trust deed for Amy drawn up a month ago, before—"

"Before you agreed to … entertain me?" He turned her way and cocked an arrogant brow.

Which meant this whole fiasco had not been so much for Amy, but for sheer revenge. He must hate her. A sick feeling unfurled in her stomach, and clenching her teeth, she held the document tight against her bosom. But hadn't she provoked him in a colossal way? She'd rushed to judgment … her actions rocked their marriage, his fortune, and his reputation.

But still he'd secured Amy's future, and Julia's, albeit via her mother's devious devices.

She ignored his query. "Explain." She wanted to stamp her foot, but she couldn't get enough traction to do it on the sandy ocean floor.

He chuckled, the sound dry as that driftwood she'd stubbed her toe on earlier. "Would you have believed me, Julia?" he bit out, his cool gaze a barrier between them.

"No." She shook her head, but she did believe now … realizing that even the eyes could deceive. At last, she understood the measure of the man she married. She wished … Breath rammed in her breast, and in a gutsy move, she crushed the wistful notion beneath her words. "It was a—"

"You'd already pegged me as a no good s.o.b."

"Y-yes." She skimmed his stern features, and dropped her gaze to the crystal clear waters. "Oh!" An unbidden smile curved her mouth in delight at the tiny fish darting by, but when she raised her eyes, he still looked grumpy. The sexiest grump … but still unsmiling.

"Yet, you included this." She waved the envelope in his face. "Drawn up between my mother and your uncle, making me half owner of the Leonadis Boat Rentals—"

He curled his lip. "Worth a mere one thousand euros at the time."

"But now worth billions."

"Yep." He shrugged.

She squinted up at him. Hmm, a little too casual … and if she knew anything about the man she married, she knew he did everything with purpose. "Why?" she asked, her words a challenge.

"You need to ask why?"

"I do." At first she'd felt bought, cheap and her pride kicked in, and all she wanted was to hurl the papers at him … and oh, yeah, skip town.

Skip town. Exactly what her mother would've done. She cringed.

This time though, she doubted he'd follow her. But after the chat with Maria, she realized a man like Michalis wouldn't shirk his responsibilities, which obviously included her. "Kinda hefty giving away half the company as a divorce settlement, even for you Michalis."

He laughed, a hard almost cruel sound.

"Or is it a one time all inclusive for spousal support?" That way he'd never have to set eyes on her again, would he?

A pang of such utter desolation washed over her, that she had to shift to get a better footing on the ocean floor. But for some perverse reason she wanted to hear the words from him.

"You'll have to figure it out," he said, tone gruff. "I'm fishing."

"No, you don't," she exclaimed. "You owe me an explanation, and you'd better deliver."

"Or?"

"Uh … the fish'll get away?"

A reluctant smile cracked his mouth, and then his cool reply nabbed the flitting amusement. "You believed what you wanted to, Julia."

"Do you blame me under the circumstances?"

148

A tug on his line intercepted his more than likely acerbic response, and she was glad of the reprieve, no matter how fleeting. The fish flip-flopped at the end of the hook, trying to escape its fate, but was no match for the man gunning the rod. As she'd been no match for the global shipping magnate, Michalis Leonadis. Rubbing her arms with her hands, she nipped her lip with her teeth, and felt her feet sinking down into the sand. This time, she'd stand her ground and do the right thing and clear her conscience.

Even if she lost him.

She'd bat the past far and away into the stratosphere … she was not Lolita. A garbled hiccup got snared in her throat. She was Julia Armstrong Leonadis. She clutched the documents in her nerveless fingers, inhaled a shallow breath, and exhaled sharply. "I'm sorry, Michalis."

He stilled, resisting the pull of the fish and … her.

The fish put up a heck of a fight, and Michalis had to concentrate not to let it get away. He grunted, every sinew in his body taut, his fingers choking the reel so hard he wanted to snap it in half. A boisterous wave swelled in with force, slamming against his legs, but he was so rigid it didn't move him, but it did her.

A surprised giggle, and she jumped the wave, missed, got splashed and rammed against him. Ocean spray spritzed his face, and his tight facial muscles began to thaw. Her giggle filled his ears, her subtle perfume … roses with ocean scent filled his senses, and he wanted to haul her into his arms.

Instead, what had he done? Punished her … but grilled himself more.

Foolish guy.

He cast her a covert glance. The waves swished against her legs, and she looked so forlorn with her cotton dress soaked to the waist, that he wanted nothing more than to tear it off her and lose himself in her.

Fueling his lungs with sea air, he blasted out an anguished sound.

He should be whipped for allowing his stubborn pride to dictate his actions, overriding his common sense to the point where he'd allowed her to go it alone this last year. And now he was nearly pushing her out the door with that sham billion-dollar deed via her mercenary mother. Since it hadn't been properly recorded it'd come to naught in a court of law. But Michalis had set the trap. He had to know.

Know the truth.

What would Julia do when she held a fistful of billions … his billions in her hot little hand?

His gut coiled inside him like a repellant. She might come to hate him anew. But to set them both free from the past, he'd had to take that risk.

Julia's mother had done a number on her, and indirectly on him. As much as he had to test her on this, perhaps more so, Julia had to know for herself. When faced with the same temptation as her mother—what would Julia do?

It was the greatest gamble of his life. He risked all … on her … on them … their future.

Never had he been so reckless with anyone, anything before he'd met Julia. Why had he behaved in such an asinine manner? He'd always been in control—then he braked, getting rammed in his solar plexus.

She'd gotten under his skin … and for the first time in his life, Michalis Leonadis couldn't control the situation, or her. And that had left him vulnerable. A growl deep in his throat cued he was still denying the revelation … the inevitable.

Julia Leonadis had become his Achilles heel.

And to have chased after her too quickly after she'd left would've spotlighted his susceptibility for a woman. He grimaced. Just like his uncle—his uncle who'd been conned by his American Lolita.

So why didn't you let her go, big guy?

Why had he concocted that ridiculous 'strategy' to bring her back to Greece with him? And then set her up—

He tightened his grip on the rod, his catch still floundering in the depths.

Time to own up, Leonadis.

He loved this woman.

He dug his feet on the sandy floor to better stabilize his footing and scratched the hair on his chest. But if he'd come out and admitted all, believing what she did about him, she'd have laughed in his face.

What's stopping you now?

Not yet, he ground between his teeth. It was her move.

Julia tucked the documents beneath her elbow, scooped a handful of sand from the ocean bottom, picked out the miniature shells, dropping each one back into the sea, and then submerged her hand, the sand washing away in the waves.

If Michalis didn't do something soon, he and all he valued most in the world would wash away with the tide. And it wouldn't matter that he'd instructed the legal whiz, Mario to draw up the real documents transferring a substantial portion of the Leonadis fortune to Julia. She'd fly back to Paris and their only connection would be Amy.

Amy, their beloved daughter.

Guilt lacerated his insides; thinking of what Julia must've gone through having their baby alone in a foreign country, when he could've provided for them both, taken care of them.

"It is I who am sorry, Julia."

Startled she snapped her head his way, her clear eyes wide with surprise, almost shock.

"I should have taken care of Amy—"

"You didn't know."

"… and provided better for you."

"I wouldn't let you, remember." She pulled the envelope from beneath her elbow and clutched it in her hand. "I won't be bought off, Michalis." She tore up the documents and tossed them into the sea.

"What have you done, woman?"

"Fed the fish?" she said tongue in cheek, then burst out laughing, the sound so carefree it wrapped around him like a long forgotten caress.

"An expensive dinner, that."

She shrugged, and studied him beneath her lashes. He remained silent for so long, she turned to go.

A beat, and he chuckled, the guilt plaguing him, dissipating in the ocean breeze. Time to stop flogging himself and set things right. For even with the Leonadis billions, he'd be a poor man indeed without his family … Julia and their daughter; the real prize was a legacy of the heart.

"Will you let me now?" A splash at the end of the line, but he ignored it, his focus totally on her. "Take care of you … you both?"

"That depends." She glanced at him over her shoulder, a glint of mischief in her eyes.

He hiked an arrogant brow.

"On how good a cook you'll be tonight."

"You doubt my skills, woman?" He played along, and shoved his hand in his trouser pocket, an indignant look upon his face.

"I don't doubt any of your skills, Michalis *mou*."

"Better," he growled, curling his fingers on the crinkled photo in his pocket. One day, they'd talk about Lolita and his uncle, but not today. Today belonged to Julia … his beautiful Julia, his wife and the mother of his child. Emotion spun into a lump in his throat, and he blinked the sea spritz from his lashes.

"But it might be a challenge even for you without the fish in the pan." She gave him a tremulous smile, and his heart boxed his ribs. Her smile turned to a laugh, and she pointed out to sea.

The big fish put up a last ditch effort, and Michalis lost his balance, reached for her and together they splashed into the sea.

He surfaced with her in his arms, chuckling. "I'm afraid, dinner's gone a-sailing." He inclined his head to the fishing pole bobbing on the surface, and the fish nowhere in sight. "But no matter" —he swept her up into his arms and raining kisses all over her face, he twirled her around to the serenade of the surf— "I've got the best catch of the day …"

"Oh, Michalis *mou*." She tightened her arms about his neck, tears brimming on her lashes and spilling over, mingled with the ocean spray on her cheeks.

"… and forever, *agape mou*," he whispered against her lips.